THEY WERE
Sisters

CONSTANCE SCOTT

authorHOUSE®

AuthorHouse™
1663 Liberty Drive
Bloomington, IN 47403
www.authorhouse.com
Phone: 1-800-839-8640

Published by AuthorHouse   11/12/2014

ISBN: 978-1-4969-5296-7 (sc)
ISBN: 978-1-4969-5295-0 (e)

Library of Congress Control Number: 2014920349

Contents

"From the old deep dusted annals,

the years erase their tales"---

And round them race the channels

That take no second sail.

A. E. Housman

Chapter 1

Ruthie Brooks stood in the middle of the road that August afternoon In 1942. She had just turned twelve. She heard her mother's cries, "Ruthie, Ruthie, don't let them take me" and watched as the Commonwealth's car pulled out of the driveway with Joan Brooks in the back seat. Two men twisted her mother's arms. Ruthie yelled, "Stop, you are hurting her." But they ignored Ruthie's pleas and forced her mother out of the cottage into the back seat of the car that was headed to Medfield State Mental Hospital in Medfield, Massachusetts.

Ruthie thought about her mother pouring hot water on the neighbor's garden. Were the neighbors really trying to asphyxiate them? That's what her mother called it. These men must be the authorities she spoke about. Ruthie began to run after the car, but a hand grabbed her shoulder.

It was Mr. Barney, their new neighbor. Her mother gave her permission to be friendly with some of the neighbors, but Mr. Barney, new to the neighborhood, wasn't mentioned. Ruthie hadn't seen him close up. Fearful, she broke free and said, "No, leave me alone, we don't know you, and my mother needs me. She's calling me. Why don't you just let me go or help me get her back?"

"The state officials said you have to come to my house and wait for your sisters. I won't hurt you, I promise," he explained. "I told the men I would take care of you. Just come to my house until we find out what else to do."

Reluctantly, Ruthie did as she was told and followed the Barney man back to his house hoping he could bring her mother back.

They entered his living room. It reminded Ruthie of her house across the street with its sparse furnishings, two rickety chairs and an old piano pushed into a corner. As she looked around, Mr. Barney said, "I just moved here––my furniture hasn't arrived, yet."

"I don't care about your furniture. I want my mother."

She watched him walk to the scratched piano. A chipped bowl containing some oranges was on top. Mr. Barney took one, turned and asked, "Would you like an orange?"

Ruthie ignored him, slumped into a wobbly chair near the door and began to sob. Mr. Barney continued trying to comfort her when they heard a soft knock. "It's my mother," Ruthie shrieked and bolted towards the door. Mr. Barney, knew it wasn't, walked over to her and said, "Take it easy, and let's just see who's there."

As soon as he pulled open the door, Beth, Ruthie's seven-year-old sister burst into the room followed by Mrs. McKinnel, another neighbor. Ruthie yelled, "There you are. Where have you been?"

"I couldn't find you and mama, so I went to the McKinnel's house," said Beth."

"I was trying to help mama. Two men in a black car took her away. If you had stayed home like she wanted; this wouldn't have happened. But no, you went to play with the McCoynes. You were gone the other time, too, when she poured hot water on the neighbor's garden. If you had been here, she wouldn't be gone, now." Ruthie started crying, hysterically.

Mrs. McKinnel kneeled down and took the little child in her arms and said, "You and Beth can stay with us until your sisters get here. They called me a little while ago, told me about your mother and said they'll come tomorrow. It'll be fun for you, and I know Sonny and Jane will like it."

"No, I don't want my sisters near me. Mama said they're dead, and that's why they left her alone. They never came to help her get food or see her, so she went without food and gave hers to us. I want to go to my mother. She needs me," insisted Ruthie.

Then to Beth, she said, "It's your fault."

Mr. Barney stayed out of the way.

"I didn't know men would take our mother," Beth said to Mrs. McKinnel.

Mrs. McKinnel gently pushed a stray hair from Ruthie's face and said, "It's not Beth's fault, and your mother is going to a hospital where they will take good care of her." Ruthie stopped crying and listened.

"But, she's not sick, and she doesn't have her magazine, the Cosmopolitan she read everyday. I know she wants it." Ruthie remembered how her mother had very little money in her small black silk change purse, but managed to feed them. She bathed them every day at the kitchen sink. First, her father was taken to prison, and now her mother was gone without the magazine she carefully laid on the sofa when she finished reading it.

Mrs. McKinnel, turned to Beth and said, "Do you know anything about this?"

"Yes, she loved books, but had none so she read the ragged old magazine every day."

Ruthie broke away from Mrs. McKinnel and lunged at Beth screaming, "You better shut up. That magazine isn't old. Mama loved it."

Mr. Barney stepped up and asked Mrs. McKinnel, "Is there anything I can do"

"No, but thank you, I know you're concerned." She took the girls gently by their hands and walked to the front door.

The three were silent as they headed up the street towards the McKinnel's home. Ruthie was oblivious to everything, because she was occupied with thoughts of finding a way to her mother.

Sonny walked towards them and said, "I heard we are having a sleep over. Great. We can play kick the can and hide and seek after supper, and then go back inside to play monopoly."

But, when they walked past the one little shack in the neighborhood where Beth, Ruthie and Joan Brooks had lived, Ruthie broke away from Mrs. McKinnel. She called through her tears, "My mother is in there, I know she is. She shouted, "Mama, mama." But, nobody answered her cries. She ran back to Mrs. McKinnel crying, "She's gone. She didn't answer." Mrs. McKinnel cuddled her, and whispered, "I'll help you. I'll find a way for you to see your mother. I'll talk to your sisters."

Ruthie calmed down, again, and said, "Do you promise?"

Knowing she couldn't promise, Mrs. McKinnel said, "I promise to do my best."

When they entered the McKinnels kitchen through the back door, Ruthie glanced around. It didn't have the same warm and cozy feeling it had in the past. She didn't like it anymore, although everything was still in its place. The bright blue walls looked gray. Mrs. Mckinnel's red-checkered apron still hung on the hook on the back of the pantry door, the teakettle was on the stove, and the air smelled like baked bread. Ruthie remembered how she had wanted to show it to her mother, but, now, it felt different. Her mother probably wouldn't like it, now.

Jane poked Ruthie and said, "Come on upstairs, and I'll show you and Beth where you'll be sleeping."

The three girls headed down the hall toward the stairs leading to the bedrooms.

As they entered a small room near the top of the stairs with white dotted Swiss curtains neatly tied back and a white bedspread with soft plush animals lying on top, Beth said, "Wow, is this where we'll sleep? I like it. I want to stay here. It smells like clean clothes."

But, Ruthie said quietly, "Go ahead. As soon as I can get across the street, I'll wait for mama. I don't care about this."

Jane said, "Ruthie, you can't. Your mother isn't there. We're taking care of you until your sisters get here."

"My sisters never took care of our mother. They're dead."

She remembered Joan's visit to a small cemetery where she had discovered a large family plot that included four graves with the words

Daughter Wellborn carved on each one. She told Ruthie they were her daughters with a new name and that explained why she never heard from them. Ruthie felt it was a mistake, but her mother seemed comforted, so she kept quiet.

"Mama must have made a mistake. Mrs. McKinnel said they are coming tomorrow."

"You lie, mama didn't make mistakes."

Jane finished showing the girls the room and then led them to the bathroom. The fussing began again.

Beth said, "Wow, look at this, a bath tub and shower. Ruthie, you know this is better. We took our baths at the kitchen sink."

Ruthie eyes filled with tears, but they didn't fall as she said, "Yes, but we had mama."

She turned to Jane knowing Jane couldn't give her permission to go home, but she felt forced to ask anyway. "Can I stay at our house across the street in case my mother comes back during the night? I don't want her to be alone. Beth can stay here and play the games with you and Sonny."

"Gee, I don't know; you'll have to ask my mother."

"Okay, I'll go down stairs."

Ruthie softly crept down the stairs and headed towards the kitchen. She remembered her mother telling her "always have a plan."

When she entered the kitchen, she smelled chicken and a cake baking. She was hungry and for a brief moment she thought about going back upstairs. Then she remembered her mother calling to her. Undaunted, she spoke.

"Hi, Mrs. McKinnel. I know you're busy, but I wanted to ask you something."

"Yes, dear, what is it?"

"May I sleep at our house tonight? That way, if my mother comes home, she won't be alone. Please, can I do it?"

"No, honey. Even if Beth went with you, I'd be troubled. Your mother won't be back tonight. I'll ask your sisters to take you to her as soon as they can."

Ruthie looked down, chewed her nail and said softly, "Okay."

She thought, "I'll find a way over there."

Chapter 2

In the evening around five o'clock, Mrs. McKinnel called Sonny, Jane, Beth and Ruthie to wash before their supper. "Mr. McKinnel will be coming up the driveway any moment, and then we'll sit down to eat."

The four went into a small bathroom near the kitchen. "Gee, "Beth said, "I didn't know anyone had two bathrooms. We didn't even have one, just a toilet."

"My father built this one so my mom wouldn't have to go up stairs all the time," said Jane.

Ruthie thought about Beth's remark. She decided if Beth said anymore about the house across the street she'd pull her hair until she screamed to make her stop. Luckily, before that happened Mrs. McKinnel called, "He's home."

Ruthie became enraged when she saw how Beth forgot all about the good times listening to the frogs at night, digging clams at the beach and their mother saving enough money for ice cream at Gus's Variety Store. She forgot her mother went without her food so they wouldn't be hungry. And she forgot her mother walked fourteen miles to get welfare money for food.

They heard the back door open with a squeak and heard her say, "How was your day?"

"Nothing unusual."

"We have Beth and Ruthie, the two little girls from across the street visiting overnight."

"Did something happen or are they just having a sleep over?"

Ruthie cringed when she heard Mrs. McKinnel tell about the state car, Mr. Barney, and the rest of the events. With these words, she heard her mother's call, "Ruthie, Ruthie, don't let them take me." She wanted to run to the McKinnels and beg them to take her to her mother and not talk about it anymore. He said in a low voice, "That's heartrending. "They can stay as long as they like."

The four children entered the kitchen. Dressed in her familiar red-checkered apron, Mrs. McKinnel bustled about serving the food. She put a platter of fried chicken, a bowl of green beans, baked potatoes and fresh rolls in the middle of the table.

Beth looked at the table wide eyed, said, "Wow, we never had a supper like this." We ate cereal, if we had milk."

Ruthie sprung at Beth, yelling, "You shut up! Stop it!" Ruthie felt the McKinnels watching and drew back.

The McKinnel family watched the commotion, finally Mr. McKinnel spoke, "Sometimes we have cereal for supper, too. Lots of people eat breakfast food in_the evening." After everyone was seated, Mr. McKinnel said a prayer. As soon as the plates were filled, Beth dug in, but Ruthie picked at hers. Sonny said, "Hey, Ruthie, you better eat or you don't get any cake for dessert."

Ruthie was quiet, but Mr. McKinnel said, "Sonny, don't be impolite."

"Well, we never get dessert if we don't eat."

Sonny's father glared at him.

"After we do the dishes, we'll play kick the can and hide and seek," said Jane.

The thought of playing hide and seek gave Ruthie an idea to look for her mother. What if she hid in her own house? Probably no one would look there, and then she'd be there in case her mother returned. Ruthie was sure her mother would come back, because she would never leave them, unless those men tied her up. The plan seemed to reassure her; she began to eat and decided to be sweet and helpful as the evening progressed, so no one would suspect anything.

Jane cleared the table with Beth's help and Mrs. McKinnel brought a delicious smelling chocolate cake and some small dessert plates.

Sonny said, "Boy, Ruthie, aren't you glad you ate?"

"I am, and it's really good, and chocolate is my favorite." She had a funny feeling in her stomach and was worried about her mother. Where was she? Did those men tie her up? How was she getting along without her magazine and us? Is she getting good food? She pushed those feelings away, comforted by the taste of the cake.

After everyone had finished eating, Ruthie said, "Thank you, Mrs. McKinnel, may I help with the dishes? I'll clear the table."

"What got into you?" Sonny asked sounding suspicious.

"Sonny, I'm not going to speak to you again about your manners." Mr. McKinnel intervened—apologize to Ruthie right now."

"Okay, I'm sorry, Ruthie."

Mrs. McKinnel said, "Everybody will help clear the table and wash and dry the dishes. I expect the kitchen to be clean before you go out to play."

All four responded, but when the McKinnels went out on the screened porch, Sonny threw the dishcloth at Jane and shouted, "You have to do the pots and pans. I did them last time."

Beth said, "Oh, oh, Sonny you're going to get into trouble, and you might not be able to play hide and seek, and kick the can."

So Sonny rolled up his sleeves, and the four the four went to work, cleaning everything, until Jane called, "Mama, we're finished. We're going to get the McCoyne kids to come play."

"All right dear, come in when the street lights go on."

When they reached the street in front of their house, the McCoynes, Jack and Marilyn, were waiting. Jack had already set a rusty can in the middle of the street and marked the bases. There was no through traffic because the street ended at a small marsh. So it was the perfect place to play. The game began and for a minute Ruthie was afraid they'd get so wrapped up in kick the can, they wouldn't have time for hide and seek. She was relieved when it ended quickly after an argument when Jack accused Sonny of not touching a base. They switched to hide and seek.

Ruthie's stomach jumped, because she knew this was her only chance to search for her mother. The six kids gathered around to choose who would be it. Marilyn McCoyne led the old jingle, "Eeney, meaney, miney, mo catch a squirrel by the toe, if he hollers, let him go. Out goes y-o-u." The letter U ended at Sonny, so he was it. He leaned against the telephone pole, covered his face and called, "Scatter."

As everyone rushed to find the best hiding place, Ruthie sneaked across the street. When she opened the screen door, she called, "Mama, mama, I'm here." There was no answer. She hadn't really expected her mother to be there, but she somehow hoped she had returned.

She quickly looked in the bedroom calling, "Mama, Mama." Still no answer. She'll be back. She loves us. She cried and rushed to the couch where Joan's magazine was still lying just where she had left it. Ruthie kept thinking about her mother but wondered what would happen when the kids found out she was gone. She knew they would look everywhere, and then tell the McKinnels. Should she worry the McKinnels? Mrs. McKinnel had said she'd worry if Ruthie went to her house. She had to find her mother even if she did it alone.

Just as Ruthie suspected, across the street, the hide and seek players slowly managed to sneak in, touch the pole and call, "I'm in." All except for Ruthie.

Ruthie heard Sonny calling and then he yelled, "Hey, everyone I have something to tell you." The group came to the pole. "I can't find Ruthie." They took turns calling, "Ruthie you're in free, you don't have to be it." She peeped out and saw the small gang run to Sonny and Jane's house for help. Sonny dashed onto the porch.

Ruthie went back to the couch with the magazine clutched under her.

Ruthie listened to some activity outside as the McKinnels hurried down the overgrown path towards the scruffy cottage by the marsh. When they entered, Ruthie heard them gasp. She figured it was the poor furniture. Her mother never let anyone in the house, because she thought they would feel sorry for them. There was a worn brown plastic couch in one corner, a warped table with a small lamp on top and an old cot jammed in a corner. But, Ruthie quickly realized it wasn't the poverty they felt saddened when they saw her curled up on the old brown plastic couch weeping and hugging the Cosmopolitan.

Mr. McKinnel approached, knelt and said, "Ruthie, you frightened us and the children. They looked everywhere for you. Sonny told us you were gone, so we came over here right away. Now, please get up, and come back to our house until your sisters come in the morning."

Ruthie stood up, and threw herself into Mr. McKinnel's arms, sniffing and crying. "No, my mother needs me. My sisters are dead. My mother said so."

Mr. McKinnel took her tiny wet hand and said, "Ruthie, there's a misunderstanding that we'll straighten out. We won't let you go if they are not your sisters. Now, let's take the magazine and put it in the room where you'll be sleeping. You can put it under your pillow, if you want. We'll get it to your mother, somehow."

Ruthie stopped crying, but clung to Mr. McKinnel as they returned to the McKinnel's house where Sonny, Jane and Beth waited. The McCoynes had gone home. Mr. McKinnel was going to help her she knew it.

Chapter 3

The next morning when Jane, Sonny, Beth and Ruthie went out to play in the backyard, Ruthie watched and waited for the sisters to arrive. Her plan was to hide in the kitchen so she could hear what they said to Mrs. McKinnel. When the car drove up the driveway, Ruthie yelled to the other kids, "I have to go to the bathroom." She left the yard.

The front door bell rang and Ruthie heard the voice of Emily say, "Hello, I'm Emily and this is Charlotte, Beth and Ruthie's sisters." In the background another voice could be heard, "Tell her we came to pick up the girls."

Before Emily answered the interruption, Mrs. McKinnel said, "Yes, come in. It's nice to meet you. I'll call Beth and Ruthie from the back yard. But, first, I think it will help if you I tell you that Ruthie has had a very difficult time since her mother was taken away in the state car. She has made at least two attempts to go back to the house across the street looking for her mother. The last time my husband and I found her weeping on the couch with her mother's magazine clutched in her arms. She kept telling us her sisters were dead."

As the two listened, it was Emily who finally spoke, "Where did they get that idea? Do you know?"

"Ruthie told my husband and me their mother had found some graves in a small cemetery where her daughters were buried. She didn't quite believe it, but it made her mother feel better, so she didn't dispute it."

Charlotte said nothing, but Emily said, "We had no idea things were that bad."

"You never came around, how could you know? We didn't even know they were without food some of the time. We didn't know anything about you, until you called, yesterday. Mr. McKinnel and I would be willing to keep Beth and Ruthie. We love them like they are ours. Beth has handled it a little better. She may be holding her feelings inside. You know how children are. It was Ruthie who was standing in the street when her mother called to her for help. They leaned on each other without even realizing it, and that helped them. I hope you can arrange for them to live together."

Charlotte finally spoke, "We've heard enough. We can take care of them, but we certainly appreciate everything you have done. If you can call the girls and take us across the street, we can get them to Quincy and try to get them settled as soon as possible."

Ruthie sensed her sisters didn't want them and were taking them because they didn't have a way to say no.

Mrs. McKinnel excused herself to call the girls. On her way through the kitchen she muttered, "Whew, what cold people. If we could just keep the girls."

She called, "Beth, Ruthie, your sisters are here."

Mrs. Mckinnel was startled when Ruthie came from behind the kitchen door and said, "I don't want to see them. They don't want us. I hate them. I don't want to go with them Beth can go if she wants to. I would like to stay here with you. You stuck up for me."

"I did what I thought had to be done. Let me call Beth and then we'll see what happens."

Ruthie said, again, "I hate them. I wish they were dead." Mrs. McKinnel gently patted her arm.

Beth came to the kitchen. Mrs. McKinnel said, "Your sisters are in the living room. They came to take you to Quincy."

"Wow, that's great. Are they really here?"

"They're waiting for you."

Ruthie said, "You're stupid, Beth."

Mrs. McKinnel said, "Shhhh." The three headed to the living room.

Ruthie exploded. "Where were you? Why did you come back? You don't want us, Mr. McKinnel is going to help us find mama. Mama thought you would come, but you never did. You're both all dressed up, and Mama had to beg for our bathing suits, because she didn't want us to swim in our underwear. She walked fourteen miles in the sun to get food. We want to stay here with the McKinnels. Mrs. McKinnel said so."

Beth watched and said, "I want to go back to Quincy. I can wait for mama to come back there."

Ruthie said, again, "You're stupid, Beth."

She moved close to Emily, "You had her taken away, Mr. Barney told me. She's not sick. She took care of us and went without food so we could have hers. Go away. Mr. McKinnel is going to help us."

Emily and Charlotte looked desperate, but Emily regained a little confidence. She crouched near Ruthie and said, "We're sorry. We do want you to come and live with us. We'll try to make you happy and let you go visit mama."

"You're sorry now, but not before, why? Mama needed you and waited for you. We don't need you now. Beth can go with you."

"Yes, we were mean, but we want to make it up to you. The McKinnels have been nice, but that's over now. You'll be coming to Quincy with us," said Emily.

Mrs. McKinnel smiled at Ruthie and winked as if to say, "Forgive them."

Ruthie finally stopped crying as she listened to Beth, "Are we going to Quincy now? Can we go to the beach?"

She studied Charlotte and Emily. They looked a little like her mother, without her softness, and they had fancy clothes and red lipstick. She always wanted to hug her mother, but she didn't have that feeling with these two. Now she had to go live with them. She felt she was going to cry, but bit her lip hard to make herself stop.

Charlotte said, "Yes. First we have to go back to the house and get the things you want to take."

"I have mama's magazine that she read everyday. She wants it. Can we take it to her?" said Ruthie.

"Yes, we can take it to her," said Charlotte. Ruthie didn't believe her, but she had reconciled that she did have to go with them and decided to figure out later how to get the magazine to her mother.

Chapter 4

The McKinnels gathered around the car that was taking Beth and Ruthie away from Huff's Neck. Mrs. McKinnel scooped Beth and Ruthie in her arms and said, "We're going to miss you. Remember, you can come and visit and stay over night whenever your sisters allow it. You'll always be welcome."

Ruthie hugged Mrs. McKinnel and said, "Thank you, I'd like to do that."

Charlotte said, "Thank you for everything. Come on girls, get into the car." Beth and Ruthie climbed into the back, turned and pressed their faces close to the rear window and waved until the McKinnels could no longer be seen.

Ruthie felt lost. If only her mother were the one taking them to Quincy, everything would be good. She looked out the window and watched all the familiar things in Huff's Neck whizz by. Gone were the days of walking along the sand, digging clams and visiting Gus's Variety Store. They'd never see Jake the fisherman who gave them free fish again. As she looked at the gulls flying around, she decided they always looked lost. Today was no different for them.

She leaned next to Beth and whispered, "I wish we were going to live together, don't you? I'd rather stay here and wait for Mama, wouldn't you?"

"Yes, but we can't. Maybe Mama will come home and take us with her."

"I hope so. She said Daddy would come back and get us, remember?"

"We'll have to wait like we waited for Mama to come back from the welfare office. We thought she wasn't coming, but she finally did come."

"Yeah, it's like that, only this seems longer."

The car stopped at a gray house and Charlotte said to Beth, "This is where we get out. Ruthie and Emily are driving on to Emily's house."

"Okay. Bye Charlotte. Bye Beth."

Emily said, "It's not so final, Ruthie. We'll see you later, Beth."

Then to Charlotte, "I'll call you after we get settled."

Ruthie said, "We'll still be able to play everyday. It's not so far."

Beth stood on the sidewalk and waved until they were out of sight.

Chapter 5

Ruthie felt unsure the afternoon, she and Emily drove up to Emily's house on Sycamore Street. She wanted to go back to the little cottage in Huff's Neck with her mother and Beth and watch the fireflies at night instead of staying here without Beth.

Emily said, "This is where I live."

Ruthie studied the brown house with white trim and small lawn. Some large trees already red and yellow from the autumn weather grew along one side. The remains of a small flower garden grew on the side of a porch downstairs that led to two front doors. How could Emily own a whole house and never come to help their mother?

"Harry, my husband, and I bought this house. He is away in the Navy for now. The house has two stories, but the downstairs part is rented to a young couple with a baby. I hope you'll like being here with us. Beth is close, too, within walking distance at Charlotte's two streets away."

"Can't we be together? Mama would want us to live with each other. Mrs. McKinnel said to keep us together. I don't want to stay here without Beth."

"I told you, we have to do it this way. Money is a problem and each of us taking one child was the best way to make it work. It was a difficult decision, but one that had to be made. Beth is close and you can see each other all the time."

Ruthie said to herself, "Emily owned a whole house and never came to see her us."

Ruthie just wanted her mother so she pretended and said, "I like it."

"Okay. Let's go in, I'll show you your room."

"Gee, I didn't know about your husband."

"I think you'll like him. He's quiet and easy going."

"He sounds nice."

Ruthie wasn't sure about anything Emily was saying, because this was the sister who signed to have her mother taken away. Now she wondered if Harry had something to do with it. She had heard Mrs. McKinnel say Emily called a doctor and signed the papers along with the doctor and Charlotte. Now she was trying to make it okay. It would never be okay without Mama. She can pretend in front of people all she wanted. Harry probably asked to go away, because he needed to get away from her.

They climbed upstairs to the second floor where the bedrooms were. "Here is yours. I'll let you get acquainted." Emily left Ruthie alone and went downstairs.

Ruthie looked at her new bedroom. She thought, again, about being back in Huff's Neck listening to her mother tell stories about eating pancakes, ham and eggs in Canada as a girl. She wanted to scream and run to the street and continue all the way to find the hospital. She covered her face in her hands and cried for her mother and Beth.

She made herself stop so Emily wouldn't hear her any noise. She said softly, aloud," I'll just look around."

This dingy beige colored room was unfriendly, but it didn't smell musty. Crooked lace curtains hung at the windows with dark green shades underneath. They were snapped to the top. Outside keeping the sun's warm rays from entering was one of the large trees she had seen when Emily's car stopped in front of the house.

Pushed against one wall was a twin bed with a worn nubby looking cover. A small white plush kitten was propped up near a pillow. The stark whiteness of the toy made the dull color of the spread more prominent. The floors had no rugs like the McKinnels. Along the wall, opposite the bed was a large closet. The doors were open exposing wire hangers hanging the length of a long rod. Some girl's clothing with price tags still on them hung from the hangers. Was it possible those new clothes were for her?

On a small table near the closet was a miniature cedar barrel made into a lamp. A brass chain hung from underneath a worn linen shade. Ruthie pulled the chain; the lamp produced a cozy brightness to the room. It felt as if it spoke, "Please stay. you'll have some happy times here." She wondered if that would be likely.

Ruthie began to snivel as she stood in the center of her new room. She wanted Beth. If Beth were here, it wouldn't be so sad and deserted. What if mama and daddy both come back? That could happen. Her mother had said her father wasn't going to be in prison forever. Her sniveling changed to sniffing. Her mother had said because people drank too much and took money that wasn't theirs didn't mean they were sent away forever. She said he'd be back to get them.

Ruthie wandered into the closet. Hanging on one hanger was a red corduroy skirt, white shirt and matching jacket. Ruthie felt the soft material, looked at the size and was thrilled. It was her size, ten. She pulled the next hanger from the rack, and read the tag, which had her size on it, too. That one was a navy blue pleated skirt with a white sweater. She touched the crisp pleats and twirled the hanger so the skirt

27

whirled around. There was another hanger that Ruthie, suddenly greedy, pulled towards her. This outfit was a red, white and navy blue plaid dress in her size. She was ecstatic. Were all of these clothes for her?

School was starting in a week. She looked at her new clothes, again, and then she ran downstairs to the kitchen where Emily was preparing supper, hugged Emily around the waist. Emily felt stiff.

Ruthie said, "Thank you, thank you for the clothes."

Emily laughed and said, "You found them, huh? Did you see the socks and underwear in that little chest?"

Ruthie said, "No, that's great. I'll go back upstairs and look right now."

She hurried taking two steps at a time. In the closet was a small maple chest with three drawers. She opened the top one and found some slips and panties. In the second one were several pairs of socks in different colors. Everything smelled new like the time she was with her mother and Beth in Grants bargain store in Quincy.

But, the third drawer held the biggest surprise, new shoes. Was she going to be the best dressed in the whole school? She was thirteen with new clothes, a new school, but no mother. Would her mother be happy for her? She imagined her mother saying, Ruthie, red looks good on you. If she saw all of the clothes, she would say, they're all nice, give Emily a chance.

Ruthie, resolute, decided to try to make the best of the whole situation. If her mother came back with her father, too, everything would be fine again. Maybe they would all live together like mama had said. They could get Beth and live like the McKinnels with a mother and a father and eat supper together every night.

Chapter 6

Ruthie went to tell Emily she really liked the clothes. Emily was cooking something unfamiliar and smelled awful, maybe boiled cabbage, but Ruthie pretended she didn't smell it, and said, "Everything is good, thank you. Is it okay if I go out around the neighborhood?"

"I'm glad you like it. Yes, but don't go far, and don't go to Charlotte's. I'll take you there after supper. Do you understand?"

"Yes, I just want to look around your yard and some of the other houses. I'll stay close," said Ruthie. She wondered why Emily sounded so firm when she said not to go to Charlotte's. What if Beth wasn't there? What if they drove Beth to some other place? The thought frightened her so she turned back and said, "Beth is over with Charlotte, isn't she?"

"Yes, but this isn't a good time to go over there. It's too close to supper. I'll take you later."

Ruthie wandered down the stairway and strolled around the back yard. It looked nicer than Huff's Neck with its flowerbeds full of flowers, Asters and big yellow Dandelions. Ruthie smiled to herself as she heard her mother say, "Ruthie, those are Marigolds. What makes them special is they bloom all summer into the fall. If you take the dead bloom, roll it in your between your fingers, you'll find seeds for another plant."

She was sad again. If only mama were here, I could hold her hand and let her show me how to roll the dead bloom. She rolled the dried flower between her fingers and found the seeds, just as her mother had said. She couldn't place the smell. It must belong only to Marigolds.

A happy voice called, "Hello, you must be Ruthie. I'm Mrs. Nichol."

Ruthie moved close to the fence and managed, "Hello."

"Emily told me you were coming. I hope we can be good friends, because I always wanted a daughter. Just call me Mim."

Ruthie was scared, but sneaked a look at the soft-spoken woman, then chewed her finger and remembered how she was frightened of that awful Dawson lady in Huff's Neck. Mrs. Dawson was nice to her mother at first, but her mother said she had spied on her at night and called her a bad name. Ruthie stayed at the fence and tried to study the gentle looking woman.

She decided she better not become involved with her, now, and said, "I hope so. I have to go. Bye."

"All right, dear, bye."

Fear over took her; she turned, ran towards the house, up the stairs and into the kitchen with her hand full of Marigold seeds.

Along the way, she felt sorry for the Nichol woman. Maybe she is nice. She has a soft face and light gray hair like the McKinnel kids grandmother. She couldn't help thinking I'll be friendly if I see her, again. Maybe she can be my pretend grandmother.

She entered the kitchen slightly breathless and said, "The yard looks pretty. I met the lady next door, Mrs. Nichol."

Emily said, "I hope you didn't tell her why you're here."

"No, all I said was hello."

"I don't want any neighbors knowing any of our business."

These words reminded Ruthie what her mother had said when the Dawson lady approached she, her mother and Beth in the yard in Huff's Neck. Her mother warned them not tell her anything. Now Emily was doing it, too. Ruthie was confused and wondered if Emily had trouble with the neighbors like her mother did. She said, "Is it all right for me to be friends with her? She seems nice. Aren't neighbors supposed to like each other?"

"I guess that won't hurt. Yes, I suppose she is nice. Just be careful what you tell her or anybody."

Ruthie decided Emily didn't like anyone. She felt that Mrs. Nichol would be a good person to know and planned to go over to the Nichols another time, and try to be friends. Emily didn't have to know everything.

Chapter 7

Ruthie wanted to see her mother before she started school so she cried and begged, "Please, Emily, let me go. Call Mr. Joyce, if you can't take me. I won't tell anyone, I promise." She figured Emily was worried about the neighbors and what they thought. She wanted to see her mother and felt Mr. Joyce would help, because he had helped before. "Please, call."

"All right, I'll call." She grabbed the telephone in an angry way and said something under her breath that Ruthie couldn't hear, clearly. It sounded like, "What a pain." If that were true, Ruthie thought this was more proof Emily didn't want her.

"Gee, Emily, I don't want to be a pest, but I want to see Mama. I don't think Mr. Joyce will mind."

She sat on the edge of a chair and waited. "You were right he didn't object. Mr. Joyce will be here this Sunday, but remember don't you dare discuss this with anyone, even Charlotte." Ruthie now wondered if there was a plan between Emily and Charlotte not to let her see her mother. Maybe they thought she'd find out something.

"Thank you, thank you. Yes, okay, I'll remember." She wanted to hug her, but remembered how she always tightened her body.

It seemed like Sunday would never arrive. When it did, Ruthie asked Emily, "Are you sure he'll be here?" so many times, Emily was irritated. Ruthie stopped asking, because Emily sighed and rolled her eyes every time. She was afraid Emily might cancel the visit when she said, "You're annoying me, now stop it."

After Ruthie dressed, she had a new set of questions for Emily. "Shall I wear this? Does it look good enough?" She had her red corduroy suit on with the white shirt underneath.

"That looks good, and your shoes are polished. You look nice," Emily said. Ruthie wondered if she meant it, because she never said anything caring. But, Ruthie brushed it away. In a couple hours she would be see her mother and give her some asters she had picked from the backyard. They didn't smell very good, except for a woodsy smell like leaves, but her mother liked purple. She had bought a small box of candy from the drugstore with some of her babysitting money. Ruthie missed the two little Johnson girls in Huff's Neck that she used to take care of once in awhile in the afternoon. The candy took nearly all of her money but it was chocolate caramels, her mother's favorite.

Mr. Joyce arrived exactly at two o'clock. Ruthie raced to the front door and called to Emily, "He's here, we're leaving."

Emily said, "Wait a minute, I want to tell Mr. Joyce something." She came into the hall, "Thank you for doing this. As long as you're with Ruthie, I feel secure."

Ruthie wondered what she meant by feel secure. Was it dangerous to go to a mental hospital? She didn't know, but was still happy about going.

Then Mr. Joyce said, "I'm glad I can do it for her. We should be back early this evening."

Ruthie and the social worker walked to his car and both sat in the front seat. Ruthie kept fixing the collar of her shirt under the corduroy jacket. After that, she fixed the jacket collar. She was nervous and excited about seeing her mother and said, "How far is it? Does it take long?"

"Oh, it's about fifty miles from here and takes about an hour," he answered.

"An hour isn't so long, is it? Fifty miles sounds far." she said.

"No, we'll be there before you know it." he said.

As they drove along, Ruthie watched the scenery mostly country with cows grazing and sometimes sheep. She thought about seeing her mother. She'd run to her and smell her powder and touch her soft hands. Maybe she could tell her mother Mr. Joyce was trying to bring her home.

She said, "Is it all right if I tell my mother you are bringing her home?"

He said, "Who told you that?"

"Oh, Emily did."

Mr. Joyce looked very serious as he ran his hand through his gray hair and said, "No, don't tell your mother that. I might not be able to do it. I'm trying to get Dr.Halton to review her case, and that isn't completed, yet. Sometimes it takes a long time. We don't want to give your mother any false hope."

"Okay, I was trying to help her. Are we getting close?"

"We're almost there. We should be at the front gate in about ten minutes."

"Gate? Is it locked? Can we get in?"

"Yes, cars can drive in, park and go to the visiting area."

Ruthie looked in amazement at all the red brick buildings and said, "Gee, this looks like the gardens at the Wilson Mansion in Quincy. "Which one is my mother in?" She spotted bars on the windows of some of the buildings. Oh, no! Why are there bars on the windows? You said my mother was in a hospital being cared for not locked up with bars. My mother is frightened. I know she is. I want to go to her." She squeezed her hands into tight fists.

"Yes, some of the patients could harm themselves so they need extra protection. Your mother is not one of them try to stay relaxed. I'll find out where your mother is when we get inside, I'll handle everything, because you are a little young to visit. I can arrange it, because I am the social worker."

"I'm worried, but I'll stay quiet. I won't let anyone see me scared."

They walked up the stairs to the red brick building with a sign that read, Administration Building over the door. Mr. Joyce opened the door, a man in a tan uniform with some kind of badge stepped forward, "May I help you? I'm the security guard."

Ruthie thought guard? Why are there guards in a hospital? The whole area smelled like pine cleaner and bleach. The walls were a dull mint green with railings attached half way up. Some other people dressed in uniforms entered the area.

"We're here to visit a patient," Mr. Joyce said.

"Over there is the admitting desk where you will be checked in."

Mr. Joyce motioned to Ruthie and said, "Don 't say anything."

"Okay, I remember."

They approached a desk where a stern looking woman lady dressed in a light gray uniform and dark brown-rimmed glasses sat looking at papers. She finally looked up and spoke in a gruff voice, "Are you here to visit? You can't bring a child under sixteen into the ward."

"I'm sorry, but I can because I am her social worker. She's here to see her mother."

Ruthie noticed everything was locked and studied the bars on some of the windows nearby. Maybe Mr. Joyce told the truth about the bars not being on all the windows. She was still scared for her mother. What if somebody tried to stab her? Maybe things would get better once she saw where her mother was. She let Mr. Joyce do the talking.

The stern lady said, "Okay. I'll approve the visit, but she can't take those flowers or that candy in any further than the area she's in right now."

Ruthie ignored Mr. Joyce and walked towards the lady crying. "Please let me take them. If your mother were here, wouldn't you like her to have some flowers from home and some candy?"

The lady softened and said, "Let me look at what you have."

Ruthie handed the little box of candy and tiny bunch of flowers. The lady shook the candy box and picked through the flowers. "All right, this time, but you can't do it again."

"Thank you," Ruthie said under her breath.

Mr. Joyce gave her mother's name and another man came to take them to her. They walked through two locked doors and down a dimly lit wide hall with light encased in wire and where a lot of doors were closed. All the doors had small windows with what looked like some kind of fencing wire inside of them.

Ruthie whispered to Mr. Joyce, "Why is everything closed up and all the windows in the doors have wire between the glass?"

"Remember what I said about some of the patients being dangerous and needing more protection."

"Will they hurt my mother?"

"No, your mother is protected."

They came to another door, the guard opened it with one of his many keys.

Another woman dressed like a nurse was at a desk. The guard told her they were there to see Joan Brooks, and they had permission to take the candy and flowers to her.

The nurse led them by a line of beds. Some were empty, others had women lying down some were reading. When Ruthie, the guard and Mr. Joyce walked though the ward some of them stared. Ruthie was frightened when one yelled, "No kids allowed." Another one shouted, "Yeah, get that kid out of here. Hey kid, go away. Someone will get you hee hee."

She saw her mother at the end near a window. She broke away from Mr. Joyce and the nurse calling, "Mama, mama, I'm here."

Her mother stood up and rushed to Ruthie who threw herself into her arms. She was different. Her hair was long and straggly and she wore a gray dress that looked too loose. Ruthie couldn't smell her powder or anything but hospital smells of bleach and probably medicine, but no powder.

Joan held her and said, "Oh, Ruthie I don't belong here. This is awful. People wet themselves and get punished because they can't get to the bathroom. They holler things that don't make sense. I have to get out of here. Tell Emily and Charlotte."

"Mama, it will get better, look I brought you some flowers from Emily's yard and some candy from my babysitting money. Mr. Joyce will help us." She couldn't trust Emily and Charlotte.

"You're sweet, you're always sweet. Thank you. Are Emily and Charlotte taking care of you and Beth?"

"Yes, Beth lives with Charlotte, but I can walk to their house, it's close. Emily bought me some school clothes. I am going to junior high."

"Gosh, I almost forgot you're reaching that age."

Ruthie said, "When you come home, we'll be together again and maybe daddy will be back like you told us."

"I hope so. I'm doing everything they say here and trying to help the others when I can. Like when I fed the hoboes, do you remember?

"I remember, Mama. Mama, look at the stars every night like we used to and I'll do it, too. That way we can be together."

"Okay, I'll do it. I think I can see them from this window." She pointed in the direction of the window near her bed.

A loud voice announced, "Visiting hours are over. All visitors follow the security quickly and quietly out of the building."

Joan refused to cry and said, "Ruthie, you're a good girl, I love you. I'll wait for you to come again. Thank you again for the candy and flowers. You remembered how I love purple. Give my love to Beth, may be you can bring her."

Ruthie buried her face in her mother's chest and murmured good-bye and said, "I love you, too. I'll bring Beth the next time. Maybe they'll let me stay longer." Ruthie kissed her mother's soft cheek and touched her hands with the faded tan. She hurried away with Mr. Joyce so her mother wouldn't see her tears.

On the way out of the ward, Ruthie realized she had a lot of questions to ask Mr. Joyce.

They walked down the same hall through locked doors following the security guard to the front entrance.

Once they reached the bottom of the front stairway leading to the parking lot, Ruthie flung herself at Mr. Joyce, sobbing and saying her tears, "I'm scared about the bars on the windows. What about that lady who said 'someone is going to get you.' Can you get my mother out of here? She's not happy. She looks sad. Please Mr. Joyce. We can go back to Huff's Neck. We won't bother you anymore if you can't get her out."

Mr. Joyce took her sweaty tiny hand and said, "Look, these things take longer than it would seem. Dr. Halton, the doctor who admitted your mother will have to examine her with the state's permission. There are a lot of channels to go through, but I'll tell you what I'll do, I'll start the ball rolling and see what happens from there."

"You will? Oh, thank you, thank," you said Ruthie squeezing his hand.

"Now, let's get to my car, and I'll take you for an ice cream. Would you like that?"

"Yes, that would be good. I didn't know some hospitals have bars on the windows. That lady who did the yelling won't hurt my mother, will she?"

"No, she wanted to see what you'd do. But there are patients who are difficult to handle and have to be restrained. There are those who would open a window if they could and might hurt themselves. Do you see what I mean?"

"Yes, I do but it's very scary. I forgot to ask you if my mother could get mail? Emily mailed her magazine to her, but I didn't see it."

"It was there on a small table near her bed."

Emily wondered if her mother still read it everyday. Maybe she should have told her mother more about Beth. That would have to wait.

They reached Mr. Joyce's car, drove out the gate with Ruthie looking back at the buildings. They were quiet as they drove the short distance to the restaurant.

Look, here we are at Howard Johnson's."

Chapter 8

As they walked toward the restaurant, Mr. Joyce suggested getting the ice cream and sitting in a booth where they could talk. He said, "We can get cones or a dish, what ever you want. It's my treat."

"I'll check to see if we can eat them in a booth when we get inside."

Ruthie felt a little queasy and really didn't want anything to eat even a hotdog, which she liked more than anything. She just wanted to hear her mother say she was doing okay, but she felt disconnected. She straightened up so she could prepare to question Mr. Joyce.

They headed to a booth near a window. The waitress approached and Mr. Joyce said, "We're having ice cream. Is it all right to eat cones here or is this area for meals?"

"No, you're fine. I'll be back to take your order."

Ruthie decided on a scoop of vanilla and a scoop of chocolate on a sugar cone. Mr. Joyce told the waitress they wanted two sugar cones with two scoops of ice cream on each, one chocolate and one vanilla." Ruthie's thoughts went back to her mother. Maybe she would like a cone. Did she ever have a treat of any kind?

Ruthie said, "Do you really think my mother can come home? If you call Dr. Halton and tell him we went to see her and she was fine, he'll listen to you won't he?"

"Ruthie, I am not a doctor and patients in mental hospitals are out of my line of work, but I can try. One thing I do know is it takes a long time, because everything has to be cleared through the State."

"What about other people like this? Can you tell me anything that could happen?"

"From my past experience in cases like your mother's, it takes a long time for these patients to be completely well again. Your mother has not reached that point yet, because she didn't even know who I was, and she ignored the fact that I had brought you to see her. I think I should tell you it will very difficult to get her released soon."

Ruthie bit her lip. "It won't hurt to try later on will it? Maybe in a few months? She knew me and told me she loved me. She asked me to come again and bring Beth."

"I can get some details on her condition in a few months. If it has improved, perhaps I can start the paper work."

Ruthie felt he was lying, but she had to go along with it, because he was the only hope she had of visiting her mother and possibly getting her out of the hospital. She remembered Mr. McKinnel telling her he would help her, but he didn't have an important job like Mr. Joyce, so that was useless. Emily would be no help, either. That left Beth, her and Mr. Joyce. What if Mr. Joyce thinks her mother will never come home? He acted like he knew some thing more than he was telling.

The ice creams came. Ruthie really didn't feel like eating, Mr. Joyce was nice to buy it, so she decided to eat as much as she could.

"Wow, aren't they big? He began to lick his so it wouldn't drip. We better eat them right away so they don't melt."

"Do you remember when my mother tried to get bathing suits for Beth and me? You were the only one who helped her. She was worried because we wanted swim in our underwear. You came the day after she called you. If you did that, I know you can help me now. My mother is not happy. Her hair is long and a little messy. She always had neat hair in a bun. She smelled like medicine instead of her nice powdery smell."

"I know that, Ruthie, but look at it this way. She is safe. I am sorry to tell you this, but it is going to take some time before Dr. Halton will look at her case. So you'll have to wait. I can bring you to visit her again and time has a way of passing quickly."

"Then you will try?"

"We seem to be back where we started. Yes, I'll try. Now let's head back to Emily's."

Chapter 9

As they came close to Emily's house, Ruthie said, "Mr. Joyce, I'm scared to see Emily. What can I do? How can I pretend that everything is okay? It's her fault my mother is in there."

"It might be difficult as you already suspect, but let her do the talking. Try to stay calm and answer any questions that she has. She has been there at least one time that I know of so she knows what the place looks like. Remember the most important thing is your mother is safe."

Ruthie wasn't sure her mother was safe. Some of those nurses were mean talking.

"Okay. I'll do that. What if she doesn't let me go back for a visit?"

"You let me handle that part of it, okay?"

"Thank you, Mr. Joyce. Thank you." She felt tears stinging her eyes, but held them back and squeezed his arm instead.

She felt tormented. She wanted to go in the house and tear into Emily. She felt like leaving Mr. Joyce, running away and going back to see her mother.

She had to go along with what he said so she could visit her again. She thought about the McKinnels and their promise to help her. Maybe if everything else didn't work, she could find a way to Huff's Neck and talk to them.

Mr. Joyce jarred her from her thoughts. He said, "Here we are. Shall I go in with you?"

Maybe that will give you some support."

"Okay, that will help."

Chapter 10

Ruthie and Mr. Joyce walked into the living room where Emily was sitting reading a magazine. Emily acted surprised that they were back from the hospital so soon. She stood up and said, "Gee, you made pretty good time. How was it?"

Ruthie was the first to speak and said, "I saw Mama and gave her the chocolates and flowers. First they weren't going to let me take them in, but the lady in front gave in and said I could. I'm glad, because she really liked them. The visit was short. Mama looked thin and she is not happy."

Emily said, "That's good about the flowers and candy, Ruthie. Nobody likes to be away from home in a hospital. I'm sorry to hear about that part."

Ruthie watched her nervous reactions and didn't believe she was sorry at all. Emily rubbed her hands together and kept clearing her throat.

She turned to Mr. Joyce. "Did everything go smoothly?"

"Yes, it went well. They let me take Ruthie in without any incident. Your mother was happy to see her."

Ruthie added, "She wants me to bring Beth the next time. She had her magazine."

Emily said, "We'll discuss that when the time comes. Thank you, Mr. Joyce. You really helped us out." Emily was stiff as if she were uncomfortable. Ruthie was sure she made a poor attempt to be grateful.

Ruthie stepped towards Mr. Joyce and said, "Thank you and hugged him around the waist."

"I'm glad I could help. Please call me if you have any questions or need anything else." Before he left, Ruthie heard Emily and Mr. Joyce whispering but she wasn't able to make out what they were saying.

Ruthie was ready to burst and lunge at Emily, but Mr. Joyce's presence had calmed her. She said, "Emily is it okay if Beth comes over for awhile so I can tell her about Mama?" Ruthie was dying to tell Beth all the details of the visit and how Emily acted when they returned.

"I guess so. Call her, and see if she's home."

Ruthie made the call and said, "She's on her way."

A short time later, Beth was at the door disheveled and sweaty from running over three blocks. She said, "Did you see her? Does she have her magazine?"

"Shhh, I'll tell you everything when we get upstairs." They went up to Ruthie's room.

They were hardly in the doorway of Ruthie's room when Ruthie said, "Oh, Beth it was awful. Mama was skinny and her hair was long and straggly. She begged me to take her out of there. I could hear people screaming and crying when I walked through to the place where Mama is––a place they call a ward."

"I should have gone with you. Maybe I could have helped."

"It's not even a hospital, it's a prison. There are bars on the windows and the doors that have windows have wire in between the glass. Emily and Charlotte lied when they said it was a hospital. It's not––it's a jail. Poor Mama, she thinks they will help her to get out."

Beth said, "What are we going to do? Can we get her out and go back to Huff's Neck?" They heard a noise in the hall. Ruthie said, "Don't say anything else, it might be Emily."

Emily burst into the room shouting, "You bet it's me. I've heard enough. How dare you accuse us of putting our mother in a prison? She is our mother, too. We had to do something because the neighbors in Huff's Neck were complaining about her pouring hot water on their garden and yelling at them."

Ruthie jumped off the bed and lunged towards Emily. "Oh yeah she's your mother. You never came to see her. She waited and waited and thought one of you would come. But, you sent the men in the black car that took her away. They twisted her arm and left me with one of the neighbors."

"Your mother has a mental problem that's why there are bars on the windows. Mental hospitals have bars to protect the people."

"Mama does not have a mental problem. Stop saying that. If she does, you drove her there. Even now you never go to see her, and you pretend like you care. Beth and I want to go back to Huff's Neck and live with the McKinnels. They said we could. They said they would try to get Mama back."

"Ruthie, you and Beth get used to it. Mama is mentally sick and needs a lot of care. Maybe someday she can come home, but not right now."

Through her sobs, Ruthie said, "She is not mentally sick. You put her in the place with bars and said it was a hospital. You never came to see her in Huff's Neck. She waited. She was hungry and begged for us."

Beth hugged Ruthie and said, "Emily, why can't you help us now? Don't you like us? Please help us to see Mama more and maybe she'll get well faster. Or, can we go back to Huff's Neck?"

"No, Ruthie is staying here and you are staying with Charlotte."

Beth sobbed and continued to plead. "You can help us now. If you help us, maybe we can forget about why you never came to visit Mama in Huff's Neck."

Emily ignored Beth's pleading. Ruthie had dried her tears and begged, "Why can't we be together? Please let us be together."

Emily's expression softened as she said, "Okay, maybe we can work that out. I'm sorry about Mama. Maybe we were wrong to do it they way it was done. All we had was the word of Dr. Halton."

She left the room.

Ruthie turned to Beth and said, "We'll have to stick together and work it out some way even if we don't live together. Hey, I have an idea. Come on. I want you to meet my new friend. I met the lady next door and she seems like the McKinnel's grandmother. We'll ask her what she thinks. Don't tell Emily."

"Wow, do you really think she can help?"

"We'll find out. She acted kind and sweet."

They headed to Mim Nichol's house.

Chapter 11

Ruthie and Beth walked through the kitchen down the back stairs, but when they reached the last step, Ruthie said, "We better go to the front door so Emily can't see us."

"Okay. Are you sure Emily can't see Mim's front door?"

"Yes, I looked out the window and it's hidden."

They rang Mim's doorbell and when she warmly welcomed them in, all their anxiety disappeared. She looked the same close up as Ruthie remembered her in the yard looking through the fence. She had soft gray hair and a kind face just like the McKinnel kids grandmother.

She said, "Hello, Ruthie who is this you brought with you? Don't tell me I can see how much you look alike; it's your sister. Come on in the living room so we can visit."

"Yes, my sister, Beth."

"Hello, Beth, I hope all three of us can be good friends. My goodness, you both have thick braids and the same blue eyes."

The girls walked down a short hallway to a room with soft chairs, a thick rug on the floor and some family pictures on some small tables. It felt friendly.

The feeling from the room gave Ruthie the spunk she needed, She said, "Well, that's why we came here, because we need a friend. You were so nice when I saw you through the fence I told Beth I thought you could help us."

Beth and Ruthie sat close on a small sofa.

"Oh, what is it, if I can help I will."

"Please don't tell Emily we came to you."

"Mim had a puzzled look on her face but quickly said, "I'll be careful not to tell anyone. I don't know Emily very well, because she keeps to herself even though I have invited her to tea. Let me get some cake for you, would you like that?"

Ruthie said, "That will be nice."

Mim came back with two plates; each had pieces of chocolate cake, two napkins and two forks.

They thanked her, but still sat close as they ate the dessert.

"Now what seems to be the problem?"

Ruthie told the whole story including how the black car came to take her mother away to a hospital with bars on the windows including how she had to stay with Mr. Barney who acted like he wanted to help them. She cried as she described listening to her mother call her and Mr. Barney wouldn't let her go after the car.

Beth patted Ruthie's hand as she said, "Now we don't even live together. We need to be together."

Mimi said, "Girls, most problems have a solution. I'll help anyway I can, and you can come to me anytime. All right? Okay, now let's take this one step at a time. I think I may be able to find out your mother's condition. Did you know I am a nurse in charge of a large rest home? I may be able to find a contact and check on your mother."

Ruthie said, "That would be so good. What we want to do is get her out and take her back to Huff's Neck where we know some people who said they would help us."

Beth added, "These people already helped one time and they said we could live with them. We want to be together and have our mother, too."

"Girls, this is not as easy as that. If it were, I would drive over to the hospital and see if I could get a release today. There is usually a lot of work to be done through the state and the doctor who signed to have your mother put there."

Ruthie said, "I could give you the name of the social worker who took me to see her, but I think he and Emily are working to have her stay there. This hospital is a jail with bars on the windows."

"Certain kinds of hospitals have those, but, let's do this, let me check and see what I find out. I think I can find out something by next week. I know a lot of people in the medical field."

Beth ran to her and squeezed her hand and said, "That would be so good. We have no one to help us anymore. Our mother did everything she could to take care of us."

"I should be able to find out how this happened. My goodness, you are so young to be carrying such a heavy load. I'll help."

Ruthie grabbed Beth's hands and they hugged each other. She said, "Thank you, Mim. We'll come back next week if that's okay."

"I should have some idea by then, but you're welcome anytime."

Mim said, "Gosh, you girls have been through a lot in your young lives, haven't you?"

Beth said, "Yes, but our mother was fun, and we had good times with her. She taught us how to swim and dig clams and she told us we could have ham and eggs if we had the ham if we had the eggs."

Mim laughed and said, "There's a lot of truth in that."

Ruthie stacked the two plates and placed them on a small table. As she and Beth rose to leave, she said, "Thank you so much, Mim. I knew I could trust you the first time I met you."

"I'll do my best, and when you come back next week, I should have found out something. Come on Wednesday afternoon after three o'clock, that's when I'm home. In the meantime just accept things as they are even though it's difficult, and we'll try to work something out."

Beth and Ruthie hugged her, said thank you and said they'd come back Wednesday. They left by the front door.

Down on the sidewalk, Ruthie said, "Oh, oh. I think I saw the shade move. Emily is watching us."

Chapter 12

After Ruthie and Beth left Mim's house, Ruthie pulled Beth by the sleeve behind a large maple tree outside of Mim's house.

She said, "I'm scared to go home, because I think I did see the shade move. Emily doesn't like me to get friendly with neighbors. I told her I met Mim and that she was nice. Emily didn't like it."

"Maybe it looked like the shade moved. I didn't see anything, but let's do this. Let's say Mim invited us in. That way it won't look like we did it ourselves."

"Good idea, it's better than trying to pretend we didn't go in her house, but I'm not going to say anything unless Emily brings it up. If she does find out, we might not be able to see each other anymore."

"I won't say anything to Charlotte, either. Charlotte seems different than Emily. She lets me talk to the neighbors. But I bet they would stick together against us."

Ruthie said, "Yeah, look at what they did to Mama. We start school tomorrow. so we will have to go to Mim's after that."

"Meet me at Emily's after school next Wednesday. After three o'clock like Mim said."

"Okay. I better be going home now."

"Yes, it's getting close to supper time and we don't want to get into trouble."

Beth walked towards the corner of the street and called, "Bye, Ruthie."

Ruthie yelled, "Bye." Beth came running back to hug her and said, I can't wait for next Wednesday." They squeezed each other and then split up.

As Ruthie walked towards Emily's house, she looked down at the sidewalk and walked as slowly as she could.

When she entered the house, Emily was breathless and her face was red said, "I have some news. Harry is coming home for a weeks leave from the Navy. I'm excited."

Ruthie was scared the news might be about the visit to Mim's, but managed. "Wow, that's nice. Maybe I can make a poster to hang up that says welcome home."

"I bet he'd like that, Ruthie. That would be nice."

Ruthie really didn't care that Emily was happy, except that Emily had her mind on other things now instead of Beth and her going into Mim's house. Maybe Beth was right, maybe the shade didn't move.

Ruthie said, "We start school Monday. What day is Harry coming home?"

Ruthie hoped it wouldn't be Wednesday.

"I'm going to meet him Monday at the subway station. He's excited and so am I."

Relieved she said, "I'll make the poster on Sunday. That will give me a lot of time to make it nice."

"Okay, but be sure to have your things ready for your first day at school. Are you going to meet Beth and walk together?'

"No, because I go to Central, remember? She goes to Massie."

"What's wrong with me, I forgot that she's a year behind you. I made spaghetti for supper, so set the table and we can eat."

Ruthie gladly moved to set the table. Her mind reeled with thoughts of what Mim would find out about her mother.

What if her mother could come home, where would they go? Maybe Huff's Neck? If not, maybe Mim could help them find a place.

Ruthie's mind turned to Harry coming home. As she put the dishes on the table, she said to Emily, "I can't wait to meet Harry. It'll be fun to have him home with us."

"You'll like him. Most people do. He's soft-spoken and very easy to get along with. And, he likes to laugh and have a good time, too."

At the supper table, Emily chattered about Harry and his homecoming. Ruthie was glad she didn't ask any questions because she was lost in the thought about Mim's help and the possibility of she and Beth living together. Ruthie didn't like the spaghetti. It had too many tomatoes in it. She remembered her mother saying a spaghetti dinner was easy to fix. Emily's must have been real easy, it was awful.

After the dishes were finished, Ruthie said, "I'm going to my room to get my things ready for school, good night."

"Oh, good night, Ruthie."

Upstairs, Ruthie sat down on the edge of the bed and thought, "Maybe Harry and I can become friends. But could he be as nice as Emily says? How could anyone really love Emily? Maybe she's different around him.

Ruthie was trying to be happy about Harry, too but suddenly she was terrified. What if Harry takes Emily's side against her mother? Meeting Mim on Wednesday was the only hope now.

Chapter 13

Ruthie was up early for her first day at school. Her thick sun streaked hair was brushed loosely with one small braid tucked hanging on one side. She chose the plaid skirt and white shirt. Her mind raced with thoughts of all the other kids having mothers and fathers. Once the kids found out she was living with her married sister, would they act different? Emily was taking her to register so at least she had somebody.

As the car approached the school, Ruthie studied the kid's clothes and decided she was dressed okay. Most of the kids had skirts and sweaters or shirts on, so Emily had done a good job picking out the clothes after all.

Emily led the way down a corridor with a wide polished wood floor to the principal's office. A few kids were on their way to classes and some were headed to the office, too. Ruthie was worried the principal might ask questions about her mother. What if Emily tells him she in a hospital and he knows those hospitals have bars on the windows. Ruthie said, "I don't want to go in there. I don't want anyone to know about Mama."

Emily said, "I'm not going to say anything about Mama. I'll handle it, it'll be okay." For once Emily acted with kindness.

Inside a small fat secretary handed them a registration form. After it was filled out, the secretary looked it over and said. "Mr. Sampson will want to talk to you, personally." She explained he always wanted to meet with guardians.

Ruthie bit her lip. She wasn't inside the building very long and already she was feeling the difference of being without her mother.

The secretary added, "We have quite a few students with guardians, so Mr. Sampson made a practice of meeting with them." Ruthie felt a little more comfortable.

Mr. Sampson, a tall skinny man with a patch of white hair on the top of his head introduced himself. He looked gentle, but had a stern voice. Ruthie knew other principals who acted the same way. She had already decided he had to act that way because he was the boss of the school. He made the interview easy, though, as if he knew Ruthie might be embarrassed that her mother was not there.

He looked at Ruthie and said, "I want you to be happy here. School should be a good experience and I try my best to make it that way. Ruthie, it's nice to have you here."

Ruthie looked down and said softly, "Thank you."

A student aide came into the office, Mr. Sampson said, "Marianne please take Ruthie around to get acquainted with our school."

Marianne said, "Hi, Ruthie. I live across the street from your house. I hope we can be friends. We'll be in some of the same classes."

Ruthie felt better and said, "That will be fun."

Once outside the office, Emily excused herself from Marianne, "I would like to talk to Ruthie. Can you excuse us a minute?"

"Sure. I'll wait over here." She moved a short distance down the hall.

Emily said, "Ruthie, you can be friendly, but you are here to learn, not fool around. Do you understand? Don't discuss any of our personal business with anyone."

"I understand. I won't tell anyone anything. I'll pay attention." Ruthie thought how glad she was to be away from Emily and her unfriendly ways every day.

"Okay. I'll see you this afternoon after school." She walked towards the exit.

As Marianne came towards Ruthie, Ruthie thought Emily acted a little like her mother about friends and neighbors. Ruthie remembered how her mother didn't want to give Mrs. Dawson at first. Ruthie had

to beg her. Emily was the same way. Ruthie had decided Emily was not

going to keep her from Mim and now it was Marianne.

Marianne approached, "Let's go to the gym first. I'll show you

where the basketball court is and where we have our gym classes."

Ruthie was confused. "Gym?"

"Gym is where we play games and exercise. The gym teacher is Miss

Willie, and she very nice. She chooses the cheerleaders, too. You'd be a

great mascot for the cheerleading team."

"Huh?"

"Cheerleading."

"Oh, yeah, we didn't have them in the grammar school I went to.

But, my friend's sister tried out for it."

The gym had a hardwood floor with basketball hoops at each end

and rows of seats on each side. It was the first time Ruthie had been

inside of a real gym. She had seen them in pictures.

She said, "Gee, this is big."

"You'll get used to it. And you'll have a lot of fun here."

Marianne continued, "We better be getting back upstairs so I can

show you your class rooms. You already know some teachers are nicer

than others. You will have a homeroom. The main room you go to every morning. After that you go to other classes. Your homeroom teacher is great, Miss Cash."

They came to a room in the corner at the end of the main hallway. Marianne opened the door and said, "Hi Miss Cash, this is Ruthie Brooks. She'll be in your homeroom."

"A young lady with long wavy hair almost able to pass for a student, said, "Come in, Ruthie. We're glad to have you."

A boy in the back whistled. Miss Cash said, "That's enough."

Ruthie glanced around the room. It had a cozy feeling with the sun coming in windows on two sides. Nature posters, mostly animals hung on some of the walls at the back. The ever-present blackboard took up most of the front of the room.

Ruthie said in a voice, almost a whisper. "Thank you."

Marianne said, "I'll see you later, Ruthie."

"Okay. Bye."

Miss Cash took Ruthie to an empty desk in the middle row. She handed her a paper with a schedule of classes and their locations typed on it. Everything was very grown up so different from the school in Huff's Neck. Ruthie glanced around the room and noticed, in particular, the boy who had whistled. The rest of the kids looked the same as those she had seen in the schoolyard.

When she met her English teacher, Miss Waddell, she felt secure. This teacher had a gentle face like Mim and soft dark hair wound in a bun like her mother. She even wore a black skirt and a dark green top like her mother.

Ruthie thought, "I'm going to love this teacher. She and I will be friends." Then she remembered Emily's admonition. Again she thought, Emily won't be around and she won't know anything about it. I'm not telling Beth or anyone. This time, it's my secret.

Besides, Charlotte acts a little different than Emily according to Beth. Beth said she doesn't mention neighbors and keeping quiet like Emily.

But, she couldn't be that different didn't she help put her mother in the prison/hospital? Ruthie was happy with the first day at school. She was happy to be away from Emily everyday for five days a week.

Maybe she would try for the mascot position.

Chapter 14

When the bell rang at 2:30 ending Ruthie's first day at Central Junior high, she was bursting with news about her experience. She thought, "If I could go to the hospital, I could tell Mama all the news. And, I could tell her about Mim, and the chance she could get her to come home."

"Hey, Ruthie, wait." It was Marianne weaving her way through the other students gathered in the hall with a struggle.

Ruthie's daydream ended. "Okay, what?" They were standing with many other small groups kids all talking in low voices. Every once in awhile a loud burst of laughter came from one of the groups. Then it would get quiet again.

"Let's walk home together. Can you come to my house? My mother makes cookies every first day of school as a treat."

Ruthie felt her heart sting, but said, "No, I have to go straight home. My sister, Emily will be waiting for me." She didn't mention that Emily probably wouldn't care about all her discoveries that day at school or that there wouldn't be any cookies waiting.

As they walked along Hancock Street, they kicked at the autumn leaves. A weak sun shone through some of the leaves still clinging to the row of maples. The smell of burning leaves drifted from some of the yards they passed.

Marianne said, "I bet it's fun living with a sister. You can get away with a lot, huh?"

"No, my sister is like a strict parent." She was afraid to say too much for fear Emily would find out she had been talking.

Marianne continued, "Where is your mother anyway?"

"She's sick in the hospital."

"Oh, I didn't know." She twisted her lip a little and then changed the subject quickly, so Ruthie figured she was embarrassed.

"You should really think about cheerleading. If you get picked, you can wear your uniform every Wednesday when they have the games. You could go to all the games on the bus with the team and get in free."

"That sounds like fun. I think I would like it."

"Oh, I know you would and I bet you will picked, because they don't have a mascot, yet. Hey, I forgot to tell you, we have a great youth group at my church, maybe you can join that and we can go together

"I'm really not sure. I want to think about the cheerleading, first. But in case, what church is it?"

"St. Anne's. You are Catholic, aren't you?"

"No." Ruthie was sure Emily would disapprove of Marianne and her church. Emily thought Catholics were phony because they went to confession every week and then came out and did the same things they had confessed.

"I like the cheerleading and the church group sounds like fun. But I'll have to think about it some more." Ruthie was afraid to say anymore than that for fear it would get back to Emily. She was sure Emily would not let her do it so she wanted to keep it a secret, and she was positive Emily wouldn't let her go to the church group.

"Why? What's to think about? Miss Cash helps Miss Willie choose the cheerleaders. Miss Cash likes you. I could tell when I took you to your home room."

"I'll have to see. I can't say yes or no right now."

They arrived at Marianne's house. She said, "Let's go for a walk in a little while, want to?"

"I can't, because I'll have to go to the store for my sister. But, we can walk to school tomorrow morning. We can talk about the cheerleading."

"Okay. Quarter till eight, huh?"

"Good. Bye."

"Bye."

Ruthie crossed the street the crisp autumn air filled her lungs. The crunch of the leaves as she walked through small piles had some red color mixed in. She saw a beautiful one, but when she picked it up, it broke in small pieces. The trees were nearly bare. She thought about the one tree outside her mother's hospital window. Without its leaves, her mother could see more of the grounds.

She walked up the stairs into the kitchen. It smelled like bleach, and Ruthie saw the curtains were down in the kitchen. She thought Emily would want her to help with some cleaning. But, instead she said, "How was your first day?"

It surprised Ruthie. Was she really interested?

"It was great. I think I'll like it. They have a gym and gym classes. We don't have all of our studies in one room. We go to different rooms with different teachers. It's so much fun to walk down the hall and see all the other kids. I think it's going to be good."

Emily said, "Harry is coming tomorrow. If you are going to make that poster, you bet get to it after you do your homework. Do you have homework?"

"No, not today."

Emily added perfunctorily, "I'm glad you like Central. It can be some of the best days of your life. I loved it when I went there."

Ruthie turned to go upstairs when Emily added, "I need some things at the store. There is a list and some money on the kitchen table."

"Okay, I'll do that right away. and then I'll get on to the poster."

Ruthie flopped on her bed and wondered again about Harry. She decided she wanted to trust him and be friends with him. Emily was nice about her first school day. Maybe things were getting better.

She changed her school clothes and thought about her mother. A guilty feeling crept into her thoughts. Was she being too happy that day?

Her mind wandered to Marianne. Ruthie didn't care if Marianne was a Catholic, but she dreaded when Emily found out. According to her there were no good Catholics, Italians or Jewish people. Emily often said, "We need to stick with our own kind."

Ruthie thought about our own kind. What kind? The kind who are unfriendly to neighbors and put their mothers in a prison hospital?

Emily called, "Ruthie, please go to the store now."

Ruthie finished changing her clothes and hurried downstairs. She went to the kitchen to get the list and money for the store. She heard a soft knock at the kitchen door. It was Marianne. "Hi, I have to go to the store and I thought we could go together."

Emily entered the kitchen. Ruthie said, "Emily, do you remember seeing Marianne in the hall the first day at Central? Well, she has to go to the store so we are going together if that's all right."

"I suppose so."

Ruthie looked at Marianne and saw the surprised look at Emily's cold response. She ignored Emily and blurted out, "Can Ruthie come to our church youth group on Sunday nights?"

"What church?"

"St. Anne's Catholic church."

Ruthie tried to give Marianne the high sign to shut up. It didn't happen.

"Listen, we have our church. If Ruthie goes to a youth group, she should go there."

Marianne said quietly, "I was trying to be friendly."

"And, I appreciate that."

Ruthie said, "Let's go to the store." Then to Emily, "I'll go get your things and come right back."

Emily changed suddenly. "I hope I wasn't too harsh, Marianne"

"It's okay, thank you."

Emily looked at Ruthie as if to say, "We'll talk about this later." Ruthie knew that would happen.

The two girls walked down the stairs to the street. The afternoon sun was going down and there was a cool breeze blowing.

Marianne was the first to speak. "Gee, your sister is mean. I'm sorry Ruthie, but she is mean."

Ruthie said, "I tried to tell you she was strict, remember? She acts worse than that sometimes. I don't think she'll let me be a cheerleader. But, I already decided I will go to the tryouts without telling her."

"Wow, what about the youth group? Can you get out for that?"

"I'll work on it."

Chapter 15

When Marianne and Ruthie reached the sidewalk, Marianne said, "Gee, I hope you don't get into trouble over the youth group."

"If I don't get into trouble for that, it will be something else. My sister doesn't like Catholics, Jews, Italians and most everybody else. She finds something wrong with just about everybody. There is a lady down the street, Mim who has been so nice to me. I haven't told Emily because I want to stay friends with her."

"Oh, I know Mim, Mim Nichol. Everybody likes her. I bet if Emily knew her, she couldn't help but like her."

"Whatever you do, don't let Emily know I told you all this stuff."

"I won't. Maybe you can sneak to the youth group. I know some other people who do it for the same reason."

"If I sneak at anything, I think it's more important to sneak at the cheerleading thing. If I do try out and get picked, I don't know how I'd get the money for the uniform."

"We'll find a way. My mother always says to cross that bridge when you come to it."

"I'm going to have to."

They arrived at the A&P, bought their things and then turned to go back home.

On the way home, Marianne asked, "What's wrong with your mother? Is she coming home soon?"

"No, she has pneumonia and they are afraid it will turn into TB. It's going to be a long recovery."

"Oh."

"But, I go and see her. Emily lets me go."

Ruthie felt awful lying but she was grateful she thought fast enough to make up such a story. She wished it were true.

It was late in the day when Ruthie entered the kitchen where Emily was having a cup of coffee. She had an angry look on her face when she saw Ruthie.

"Listen, don't you ever dare bring another kid in here who has the nerve to invite you to a Catholic church. Catholics are phonies. They do all kinds of things, go to the priest and confess and then go back and do them again."

"Marianne has been very nice to me. I don't think she does that stuff."

"Oh, yeah, then that's unusual. Anyway, you aren't going so don 't even approach the subject."

Ruthie became very brave and alleged, "You're treating her like Mama treated Mrs. Dawson before she found out Mrs. Dawson was nice. I'm lucky to have a friend who goes to the same school living right across the street. Maybe if you knew her, you'd like her."

"Okay, you can be friends with her, but forget any socializing at the Catholic church."

"I will."

Emily began to put the groceries away.

Upstairs in her bedroom, Ruthie began to think about her mother and how much she wished she were still in Huff's Neck in the shabby little shack. She thought how they went without food, but it was better to be with Beth and her mother than live with Emily who seemed mad all the time.

She tried to cheer up by thinking about her visit Wednesday with Mim and Beth.

She hoped Mim could get her mother to come home.

Her mind skipped to the cheerleading. I bet Mim would help get the uniform money.

She wondered if Wednesday would ever arrive. She walked across the bedroom and glanced at the tree outside. Her mother had a tree that she could see through the bars.

Chapter 16

In the Morning Ruthie met Marianne outside her house so they could walk to school together. Ruthie was upset that it was a drizzly morning and her hair was hanging loosely. It looked disheveled in her tiny pocket mirror. She heard Marianne say, "Hi, we're a little bit early so we won't have to walk as fast."

"Good. Does my hair look awful? I had some curl in it, but the drizzle took it out."

"Naw, it looks good. I wish I had hair as thick as yours."

Ruthie changed the subject. "I decided to try out for cheerleading. I hope it isn't tomorrow afternoon, because I am going to Mim's house with my sister, Beth."

"Oh, I didn't know you had a sister."

"Yeah, she is still in grammar school, the sixth grade. She goes to Massie."

"Anyway, the tryouts will be Thursday afternoon at 3 in the gym. I'll meet you there."

"Listen, Marianne, don't let Emily know about this. She might not let me visit my mother in the hospital if she finds out I sneaked."

"No, I won't say anything. I can't wait. I have a feeling you'll be picked. Don't worry about the uniform. It's just a maroon skirt and yellow sweater with the letter C stitched on the front. I don't think it will cost very much. But, aren't you going to have to tell Emily, because you'll be wearing the uniform every Wednesday."

"I think I'll tell when and if I get picked."

"I'd let you have my old one, but you are so tiny."

Marianne was taller and stockier than Ruthie. She wasn't fat, but Ruthie was very petite.

Marianne had light thin hair and brown eyes. She was around 5'1" and Ruthie was just 4'11."

"Hey, that's an idea maybe I can have yours altered."

"No, it wouldn't work, because you would still need a sweater. I am sort of chesty so you couldn't wear mine. We'll work it out."

As they walked closer to the schoolyard, the sun poked through the drizzle.

Ruthie said, "Wouldn't you know the sun would come out after my curls are wrecked?"

"That always happens. You know how you said Emily is strict and sometimes mean?"

"Yeah?"

"My father is too. He gets home from work early sometimes, and I dread it. He makes me do all this extra housework and my mother doesn't like the way I do it. It causes a problem for all of us. Sometimes I feel like I don't like him at all even though he is my father."

"Well. I could have that same problem. How would you like to be me? I don't even know Emily's husband, Harry. I'm just hoping he is a nice man and that he likes me."

"I think I saw him before he went in the Navy. He helped me with my dog, Queenie. He seemed friendly and nice."

"I hope you're right. It would be lucky for me. Queenie comes up to me and drops a rock whenever I see her."

"Yeah, that's a present or you. She's the neighborhood pet."

They approached closer to the school. Cars were going in and out of the parking lot. Parents were dropping off kids. The bell rang signaling five minutes to get to homeroom.

Ruthie said, "I have to get moving. My room is further than yours. Hey look, there's that cute boy in my homeroom. I'll see you at lunch."

"Okay. Don't mention anything we talked about."

"I won't."

They hurried in opposite directions along with a crowd of other kids anxious to get to their homeroom before attendance was called.

Ruthie made it just in time.

Miss Cash said, "Ruthie it might be a good idea to get here a little earlier."

Ruthie said, "I will." Then she wondered if that would have any affect on being picked for cheerleading."

Chapter 17

On Wednesday, Ruthie was so wound up about going to see Mim after school, she was afraid Emily might notice that she was more bubbly than usual.

At breakfast, she said, "Emily, Beth is coming over after she gets out of school. Is that okay? We are going to Marianne's house to play a new game that she has."

"Yes, that's fine. I think Marianne's family has kids over there all the time. I guess they have fun."

"Yeah, her mother is really nice."

Ruthie looked at the clock, which was nearing eight thirty. She stood and took the breakfast dishes to the sink.

Then turned to Emily and said, "I have to go, Marianne will be waiting to walk to school, Bye."

"Okay, bye. Have fun after school."

"We will." Ruthie was so keyed up about Emily being nice and going to Mim's in the afternoon, she didn't even think about lying again. All she did lately was lie and sneak. She did think. She thought, what if Mim did succeed in getting her mother to come home? Would Mim be able to find a place for her, Beth and her mother to live?

She decided to wait and see what Mim had done. Even though it was a cool autumn day, her hands were sticky thinking about the possibilities.

Marianne was waiting in the familiar spot under the big tree in front of her house. Queenie did her ritual and rushed to meet Marianne and dropped her now familiar rock for her gift.

Ruthie said, "Hi, Queenie, thank you."

Then she quickly approached Marianne and said, "Marianne, I'm going to Mim's after school with my sister, but I lied to Emily and said I was going to your house, is that okay? You can't tell anyone, please."

"Yeah, that's okay, but what if she comes looking for you?"

"Can you tell her that I haven't gotten there and that I must have gone to meet Beth?"

"Okay, that's a good idea."

They were nearly at the ball field at Merrymount Park, halfway to the school.

"How come you're going to Mim's anyway? Why is it such a big secret?"

"Well, Mim is a nurse and has an important job in charge of some rest home. She knows a lot of people, and I asked her to see if she can get my mother to come home. Oh, I told you how Emily acts. so I had to sneak."

"Gee, you're sneaking a lot. You're going to get caught on something. I hope you can remember all of it."

"I know it, but I'll have to take chances. You will help, right?"

"I will, and I won't tell anyone."

They crossed Hancock St. at the football stadium and decided to walk faster so they wouldn't be rushed. When they arrived at the schoolyard, it was crowded with other kids, carrying lunches, books and hurrying towards the buildings. Some in pairs stopped to tell kid secrets.

Ruthie said, "Hey, don't wait for me after school, okay? I have a dime, and I'm taking the bus home so I can meet Beth. I'll see you at lunch and tomorrow morning. Don't tell anything I told you to anyone."

"I won't, see you at lunch, bye."

"Bye."

Ruthie was the happiest she had been. She was sure Mim would have good news. She rushed to her homeroom and said, "Hi, Miss Cash, I'm earlier today."

"Great, you seem very excited. Anything you want to share?"

"No. I just think it's going to be a great day."

Two thirty finally came. As soon as the bell rang, Ruthie rushed down the hall before the crowds and ran across the campus towards the bus stop. It seemed like the bus was slow getting there, but it actually arrived in time for Ruthie to get to Wollaston to meet Beth.

When the bus pulled away from her stop, Ruthie hurried to the big maple tree outside Mim's house. Beth wasn't there. She had a new set of problems. What if Beth forgot? What if something happened to her? Then she saw her hair flying in the wind as she ran towards Ruthie.

Ruthie said, "Gee, I was afraid something happened, and you weren't able to get here."

"Naw, it was just the class getting dismissed a little late."

They hurried up on Mim's porch and rang her bell.

When she opened she door, Mim said, "Hi, you two, don't you look nice? I've been watching for you so we can have our talk, come in."

They went into the living room where cake was set out in two plates with a small glass of milk beside each one.

Mim invited them to sit on the couch made to accommodate two adults. They thanked her and sat down.

Ruthie spoke first, "Did you find out if our mother can home? When is she coming? Can you find us a place for the three of us to live?"

"Hold on, one thing at a time, Ruthie. First, I spoke to many people and attempted to get the answers you're looking for, but it's not possible right now. The doctor who signed the paper for her to go there said she is not ready to be released. I'm so sorry. I dreaded to tell you girls this. But the positive side is that your mother is getting better. We have to be patient."

Ruthie cried, "Let me talk to those people. Take me to the hospital. I'll talk to the lady who said I could take the flowers and candy to my mother. Maybe she can help. I want my mother, she needs us."

Beth, although two years younger shed tears, too, but tried to comfort her by saying, "Ruthie, don't cry. We'll have to wait for mama like we did before. She'll come home. Remember she always came home when we worried about her trips to get food?"

Mim squeezed onto the little couch and said softly, "When the time is right, these things work themselves out. I have seen it in my work over the years."

Ruthie settled down and answered, "Thank you Mim for trying. At least we can talk to you, and you know about our mother." Ruthie began to feel good inside. She had someone she could trust and who understood.

"As I said, we have to be patient and wait a little longer. Now, let's please tell me about your school while you have your cake."

Ruthie asked one more question, "Mim, Mr. Joyce wasn't one of the people you spoke to, was he? We think he plans stuff with Charlotte and Emily."

"No, I remembered you mentioned something like that so I was careful not to let him find out anything, even some of the ones I contacted mentioned that I call on him. I didn't."

Ruthie reached out and squeezed Mim's hand in response and said. "Good, then he will still take me to visit and maybe Beth can come, too."

Beth said, "Can you take us, instead?"

Ruthie said, "What a good idea, can you? Can you do it this Sunday?"

"I don't know about that. Won't Emily have to be told?"

"Yeah, we'll go with Mr. Joyce."

Beth said, "I have to go, Charlotte will be looking for me."

They stood up, thanked Mim again. Ruthie kissed her cheek and Beth put her arms her waist affectionately. They left her and the half eaten cake.

Chapter 18

Ruthie was quietly disappointed that Mim was not able to get her mother released. She kept it from everyone except Beth and Mim.

She decided it was no use to keep prodding Mim to try anymore. For now, the visits would have to be enough. What if she told her mother someone, an important nurse, who knew people might get her home? Maybe that would make her mother happier. She decided to do that and to tell her mother at the same time that she was going to try out for cheerleading, too. She had so much news she wondered if she could wait until Sunday for the next visit.

It was arranged. Mr. Joyce was to pick her and Beth up on Sunday at 2:30.

Ruthie had told Beth, "Don't say too much of anything in front of Mr. Joyce.

He acts nice and like he can be trusted. Remember I heard him whisper to Emily?"

Beth said, "Yeah, I remember. I'll watch everything I say."

The weekend finally came.

Sunday afternoon around 2:15 Beth came to the door. Ruthie yelled to Emily, "It's Beth. I'll get it."

Emily came into the hall, anyway and said, "Hi, Beth. I guess you're pretty excited, huh? You look nice."

Beth said, "Thank you. Yeah, I am excited. I feel a little scared, though."

Ruthie said, "Don't be scared. It'll be easier because both of us will be there."

"Look, I brought some candy. Do you think they will let me give it to her?"

"Well, you might have to beg. But, the last time it worked for me."

Emily said, "Just behave so you can visit."

"We will."

Ruthie looked at the clock just as it chimed 2:30 and then the doorbell rang. She jumped up and said, "It's Mr. Joyce. Emily, we're leaving." Emily had gone to the kitchen.

She called out, "Wait, I want to talk with Mr. Joyce."

Ruthie poked Beth as if to say, see?

It was Emily who let Mr. Joyce into the living room.

She announced, "Ruthie, you and Beth go into the hall while I speak to Mr. Joyce a minute."

The girls did as they were told.

Once in the hallway, Beth said, "I see what you mean. I wonder what she is saying?"

"I don't know. I can't find out."

Just as they tried to listen, Mr. Joyce came into the hall and said, "Are you ready?"

At the curb, Ruthie said, "Is it alright if we sit together in the back seat?"

"Yes, that will be fine."

The two girls climbed in the back. Mr. Joyce climbed in the driver's seat and started the car.

Beth was the first to speak. "Is it alright if I bring this box of candy?"

"I'm not sure. The receptionist didn't want to let Ruthie take anything in. But, then she gave in. So, all I can tell you is to try."

As they drove along, Beth asked the same questions Ruthie had done on her visit.

"Does it take long?"

"About an hour."

The car whizzed by pastures of cows and goats.

Beth said, "Oh, look, goats. I love goats. I wish I had one for a pet."

Ruthie said, "Goats aren't allowed in the city."

"I know that, but if they were, I'd like to have one. A black and white one."

"The kids would make fun of you all the time."

"Who cares? It would be my goat. They don't have to go near it."

Mr. Joyce said, "Beth, you sound like what other people think doesn't bother you. Is that right?"

"Most of the time."

'That's a good way to feel. Sometimes listening to others can get you in trouble."

They drove through the gate.

Beth glanced at the large expanse of lawn and gardens in front of lots of red brick buildings.

She said, "Gee, this place is big. It doesn't look like the hospital in Huff's Neck." Then she saw the bars on the windows. She cried and punched the back of the driver's seat.

"This is awful. You get my mother out of here. Bring her back with us. This is a jail just like Ruthie told me. I didn't believe her, but it's true." She sniffed and cried.

Ruthie told her what Mr. Joyce had said, "It's not that bad, Beth. It looks bad, but some of the people are dangerous and they have to be protected."

Ruthie squeezed her hand.

Beth was still sad and weepy as they got out of the car and headed toward the main building.

Mr. Joyce said, "Let me do the talking, because you're both under age."

Ruthie said, "We will."

The three of them walked under some huge trees toward steps leading into one of the buildings.

Beth said, "I'm scared. What if we get hurt?"

Ruthie said, "I had the same feeling when I came before. This is what they call the administration building. Last time there was a grouchy woman here. But, she let me take my candy in after I begged her. You might have to do that, too."

When they walked through the door, the man with a badge, a mad look on his face and lots of keys said, "May I help you?"

Mr. Joyce said, "We're here to see a patient."

"Over there," he said pointing to a desk where a gray haired lady in a green uniform sat.

Mr. Joyce approached the woman and said, "We're here to see Joan Brooks."

The woman said to Beth and Ruthie, "See those chairs over near the window? Well, go over there and sit down while I speak with this gentleman here."

Beth and Ruthie did as the woman said. On the way Ruthie whispered to Beth, "More secrets." Almost as soon as they were seated, Mr. Joyce walked towards them. He knelt, took their hands and said, "I have something to tell you. You have to trust me on this."

Ruthie jumped up and said, "What? What is it? Is it Mama?"

"Yes. Your mother died when we were on our way here. The nurses and doctors did everything they could to help her. She refused to eat, became weak and caught pneumonia. She died peacefully in her sleep."

"No, she didn't. I want to see. Show me her things and her bed," Ruthie shouted and grabbed Beth. They clung to each other.

Beth said, "Take us to where she was. Maybe there is a mistake. Maybe it was somebody else's mother."

Mr. Joyce put his arms around the two small girls and rocked them a little, then said, "Let me see if we can go to her place."

He walked over to the desk and spoke. Beth and Ruthie could hear him pleading and finally the green uniformed lady said, "I am breaking the rules, but go on with the guard."

She called to the man with the keys who said, "I'll do it, but it's against my understanding of the rules."

He led the three of them down the hall through two locked doors.

Beth and Ruthie were quiet, convinced there was a mistake. Ruthie said, "They must be wrong." They arrived at a nurse's station, which was big enough to hold a desk, chair and a few shelves. A little lady dressed in white with a bunch of daisies pinned to her pocket came from behind the reception desk, took Beth and Ruthie by the hand and led them to the area where their mother's bed was. On the way, the nurse told them, "Your mother was my favorite. She told me all about you two and how you went walking to the beach and swam and waded in the water. Here we are."

They walked through a line of beds where other women were sitting reading and watching them. Everything was white and clean. The beds were close together. Most of the people just stared. One shouted at the nurse, "Who are those kids, are they yours?"

The nurse smiled and said, "No, they are visiting. I'll tell you about it later." The woman settled back into her chair.

Mr. Joyce, Beth, Ruthie and the nurse came to a bed with a mattress rolled up near a window with a tree outside. Their mother's magazine, her powder and comb and brush set were lying beside the mattress roll. A bouquet of dried purple asters was placed near the other things.

Ruthie threw herself at the mattress and cried, "Mama, mama, you kept my flowers. We are trying to bring you home."

Beth followed, dropped on Ruthie's back and sobbed, "Please, bring our mother. We are getting help for her."

The nurse stepped up, gathered Joan's things and said, "Girls, I am so sorry. But your mother loved you very much and talked about you every day. She helped other people and was really trying to get well. She caught pneumonia and was not able to recover. I wish it were different."

She turned to Mr. Joyce who was standing out of the way and said, "We have contacted the older sisters and they are making arrangements."

Mr. Joyce knelt again and tried to comfort Beth and Ruthie. "Come now girls, gather your mother's belongings, and let's head for my car. Things will work out. Your sisters will help you through this."

Beth turned to the nurse and said, "Would you like these candies? They were for my mother."

On the way back through the locked doors, Ruthie gasped through her tears, "We wanted to bring our mother home. If you had let us, she wouldn't have gotten pneumonia. You could have helped us more. Instead, you kept secrets with Emily and Charlotte."

"Now Ruthie that is not true. When Emily and Charlotte and I spoke with each other it was always about protecting you during your visits. They didn't want to have you see anything at the hospital that wasn't necessary. Maybe it seemed like secrets, but that wasn't the case." He ran his fingers through his hair and fixed his tie. "I have become very attached to you and if it's alright with you, I'd like to stay in touch."

Ruthie looked up and said, "Mama is gone."

Beth said, "I didn't even get to see her one last time."

"Girls, your memories of her will be good ones. Even the nurse with the daisies was kind and liked your mother very much. That tells me, your mother probably got some special treatment that the others didn't get. So it's comforting to know the people here did everything they could to save her and help her. You could not have done anymore if you had her at home. You will understand what I mean some day."

Ruthie took Beth by the hand and pulled her close. "One thing we can do is ask Emily and Charlotte if we can live together. Can you help with that? If we're together like our mother wanted, we can help each other and maybe it won't be so bad."

Chapter 19

On the way to Emily's house, Beth and Ruthie sat close in the back seat. Ruthie figured sitting close might squeeze out the sadness.

"Mama taught us how to dig clams? We walked along the shore, and when a squirt came up, we stopped and dug the sand away and there they were, just like she said. We'll never go to the beach with her again, she said as she began to cry."

Beth said, "We can do that again, can't we, Mr. Joyce?" Beth seemed to be focused on the beach more than their mother dying. It made Ruthie remember all the times Beth was never around when their mother needed help.

"Yes, I think you'll be able to do that, again. It will take time for everything to settle down."

Ruthie said, "If we can live together, won't that make things easier?"

She hugged Beth and said, "We can listen to the crickets and watch the fireflies in the summer. Emily has a screened in porch where we can sit."

Mr. Joyce said, "It probably would help to ease things, but we'll have to work on that."

"You mean, you'll help us?"

"I'll mention it, but the decision rests with your sisters. I think it would be the right thing to do for you, and I'll be sure to tell them that."

His car stopped at Emily's house where other cars had gathered including Mim's and Charlotte's.

Ruthie looked at the parked cars and said, "Oh, look Emily and Charlotte are there. We can find out if we can live together, now, can't we? Charlotte and Emily are here. Please, can you do it now?"

Beth remained quiet.

Mr. Joyce seemed to take his time getting out of the car like he didn't want any confrontation, but he said, "Let's just see how things are once we go inside."

Ruthie, Mr Joyce and Beth walked toward the front door. The weather had turned a little cooler. Beth and Ruthie carefully carried their mother's pitiful possessions that were so valuable to them. Ruthie whispered to Beth, "Keep the magazine flat." She reached towards

Beth, took the magazine and tucked it under Beth's arm, making it flat. Ruthie carefully held the dried asters so the breeze wouldn't hurt them and the silver brush and comb she held in her other hand in the bag the nurse with the daisies had given them.

Emily answered the door and scooped Beth and Ruthie in her arms. She actually hugged them close. They both leaned into her arms. Charlotte and Mim were sitting near a window in the living room.

Ruthie wept, "Mama is gone. Her bed was empty, but the flowers I gave her were lying there, see? The nurse said Mama helped the other people and that she was her favorite."

Beth cried, too, "I have her magazine. The nurse said she died, but we didn't see her. Please, Emily let us live together so we can make Mama's wish come true. Mama always told us to stay together."

Emily cried and said through her sobs, "I should have helped her more, so maybe we can make up for that. We were talking about it just before you came. Beth will spend the rest of the nights here with you until we take care of the permanent arrangement in a few days." She took them by the hands and continued, "Things will get better. I'll help you."

Emily, in tears, turned to Mr. Joyce, "Thank you for helping them. It must have been difficult."

"Yes, I actually pretended I was related to them as I explained what happened to their mother. But the nurse in the ward made it a little easier with her kindness. She was complimentary about Joan and gave them a bag to put her possessions in. They were able to have those things and that helped, too."

Charlotte and Mim got up and came to embrace the two young girls.

Mim spoke first. She gently took Beth and Ruthie into her arms and said, "It's a sad time. But, the three of us will be great friends. You can visit me anytime, and I'll help you through this."

The girls nodded. Ruthie was relieved, now they wouldn't have to sneak to Mim/s house.

She kissed her cheek and said, "Thank you, Mim. Can you be our pretend grandmother?"

"Of course, that would make me very happy."

Charlotte cried hard as she went toward the girls.

Beth said, "You didn't tell us she had pneumonia. She died from pneumonia."

"Emily and I didn't find out until it was too late. But, we want to take good care of you like Mama would want us to do. We are arranging it so you can be together."

"Can we keep her things?"

"Yes, put them in a safe place."

"Is it alright if we go upstairs to Ruthie's room? We'll find a safe place there."

Ruthie whimpered, "Could they have made a mistake at the hospital? There were a lot of other ladies in there. Did you check to make sure? I wanted Mama and maybe Daddy and Beth and I to live together. Get Daddy, he'll help."

Emily said, "Daddy is on his way here."

"When is he coming? Mama was right. She said he'd come back. Maybe we can go live with him."

Emily knelt down, "Girls, listen. This is sad for all of us, but let's try to take one thing at a time. For now, you and Beth are staying with me. First, the hospital didn't make a mistake. I wish that were what happened. Now, you and Beth go up to your room. Maybe you can play monopoly for awhile."

The two girls headed up the stairs still carefully holding their mother's possessions.

Ruthie said, "We'll find a safe place for these."

On the way upstairs, Ruthie squeezed Beth and said, "Yippee, Mama, got her wish."

Chapter 20

The day after her mother died, Ruthie was in the kitchen at breakfast with Emily and Beth.

Ruthie said, "Emily, what shall Beth and I wear to the funeral home tonight?"

"You don't have to be bothered worrying about that, because Charlotte and I have decided that it won't be a good idea for you and Beth to go. You should remember mama when you had the good times with her. You don't want to remember her dead, do you.

Beth spoke. "I want to go. What if it isn't our mother? We can find out for sure."

Ruthie listened and said, "That's right. Please. Emily, let us." She wrung her hands as she spoke.

Beth said, "Please, we want to see her," as she twisted her hair.

"There is no mistake. I wish I could tell you that, but I can't. It just isn't a good idea for you two to see Mama lifeless."

Ruthie held back tears, and pulled her lips back and rubbed her chin, lightly. She couldn't picture her mother lifeless.

Beth sniffed and wept openly.

Emily added, "Besides, Daddy is expected today. You can spend the time with him. He will be at the funeral home for a very short time. I don't want you to bring this up again."

Ruthie continued, "Where is Daddy going to live? Can we go to live with him?"

"I am not going into that again. I have no idea where he'll live, but I can tell you it won't be here."

Beth said, "Why? There is an extra bedroom."

Ruthie gave Beth a signal by making a face telling her to back off. She drew her lips back and shrugged her shoulders.

Emily responded for all of them, "I am not going to dignify that with an answer." She left the kitchen.

Ruthie turned to Beth and said, "Let's ask Harry. Maybe he'll help us."

"Okay, but how can we do it without Emily around?"

"When he goes to the garage, we'll go in there after him. Now, let's clean up the dishes and get dressed so he doesn't get out of there before we can catch him."

Beth washed the dishes and Ruthie dried them and put them away. Beth said, "Do you think mama would want us to go to the funeral home?"

"Maybe not. But, we have to try one more time to make sure it's her. There were so many women in the hospital, they could have made a mistake like you thought in the beginning."

"Yeah. We'll ask Harry."

They went upstairs to Ruthie's bedroom. There was a new twin bed with a white spread beside Ruthie's bed.

Ruthie squealed, "Look, you are going to live here. Here's a bed like mine for you."

She went to the closet where Beth's clothes were hanging and saw Beth's clothes mixed in with hers. She said, "Oh, no you don't."

Beth said, "Don't what?"

"You don't put your stuff in with mine. We each have one side of the closet. It's big enough."

Beth lunged at Ruthie. "You shut up. I didn't do it. Charlotte must have brought them. I didn't even know they were here."

"Well, just remember, you have that side of the closet pointing to the left side and this side is mine so start moving your stuff."

"Okay, I'll get it done. Stop talking about it."

Beth said, "Ruthie."

"What?'

"What shall we do about Daddy? Shall we ask him if he can get a place for the three of us?"

"We'll talk about that later. First let's go to he garage and find Harry." Harry had come home on a thirty-day leave from the Navy. He spent a lot of time polishing his gray coupe and tinkering with it's motor. He could often be found in the garage.

They hurried quietly downstairs through the kitchen and down the back steps into the garage.

The garage smelled like wax and a car engine. Harry was there waxing his coupe. The garage was neat with oilcans lined up on a shelf near some wax and polishing cloths.

He said, "Hi, girls, what's up?"

"Well," Ruthie began, "we were wondering if you could ask Emily to take us to the funeral home tonight."

"I take it she said no, right?"

Beth said, "Yes, but we want to make sure the hospital didn't make a mistake. There were a lot of other mothers in there."

"No, that's not possible. I was the one who took the call from the doctor in charge at the hospital. It was your mother. I'm sorry about the funeral home. I have to respect Emily's wishes. If I go against her, it might not work so I have to go along with what she has told you, which I assume is no."

Beth looked down, twisted her lip and said softly, "Alright."

Ruthie said, "We won't ask again."

They left the garage and went back to their bedroom to find a special place for their mother's last few possessions.

Ruthie said, "We can put the magazine in here." She pulled out a little drawer in the chest in the back of the closet. "And then I'll put the asters on top with her powder beside them."

"What a great idea," Beth said. "How did you figure it out?"

"Nobody goes in it, but us, so nobody will touch them."

She smoothed out the magazine and carefully laid the dried asters and powder on top.

She started to cry," This is all we have left of mama."

Beth leaned towards her, hugged her and said," No, remember Mr. Joyce told us we could think about all the good times we had. Mama didn't want us to be sad." "Yeah, I guess you're right. At least we have these and we can come in here and look whenever we want. We can show them to Daddy. Now let's make a plan for seeing him."

They lay on their beds and planned how to ask him to find a house and take them with him.

Ruthie said, "Hey, I have a great idea. We'll take Daddy to Mim's house and maybe she can find a place for the three of us. Mim can do everything."

"Wow, how did you think of it?"

"Oh, I don't know. I was thinking about if we had a best friend who could help us.

I thought about Mim saying, 'We can be friends.'"

"It's great, we'll do it."

Chapter 21

Later in the afternoon the day Joan Brooks was at the funeral home, Beth and Ruthie decided to visit Mim to attempt to make plans for bringing their father to her house.

Shouting between a man and Emily coming from the kitchen interrupted their plan.

They ran down the stairs and into the kitchen. Ruthie ran into the area first into the arms of their father who pulled Beth towards him, too. Ruthie said, "Daddy. Daddy Mama said you would come"

Beth said, "We knew she was right. So we waited like she wanted us to do. Can we live with you?"

"Did you check to see if she is really dead or if it was a mistake by the hospital?" Ruthie folded her hands and pressed them into her chest and added, "I hope you did, but even if it's true that she died, you'll take care us, now, won't you?"

Emily answered for Tom Brooks, "No, he won't. You two are staying here. I thought I had warned you not to mention this again."

Tom said, "Girls, maybe Emily is right. Let's see how things go for now. Right now, it's wonderful to see you and how you have changed. You're growing up."

"No thanks to you," Emily added.

Tom turned to her. "Emily, please not in front of the children."

"Why not? You're responsible for putting our mother in a mental hospital. You drove her there."

Ruthie started to cry and holler. "He did not. I was there the day the men came and took Mama away in the black car. They left me alone with that Barney man. The one I didn't know. Then Mrs. McKinnel told me you signed the paper to take her away. Daddy was in prison and couldn't sign it."

Beth cried and clung to Ruthie saying, "Ruthie is right. I heard Mrs. McKinnel."

Tom gathered the distraught girls in his arms, "I'll be close from now on when you need me. Please don't cry. Let's walk to Wollaston and get ice cream in Brigham's."

Emily continued her tirade. "You get out of here. Stay away from them. You are not taking them anywhere."

Harry came into the kitchen. "What's going on here? Emily stop it. If Tom wants to take his daughters for ice cream, let him do it."

Ruthie whispered to Beth, "We can go to Mim's on the way."

Tom said, "Thank you Harry. Come on girls. He took them by the hand and led them out the back door.

Ruthie hugged his arm and said, "We knew you'd come back."

Beth added, "It's true. Mama said so."

They heard Harry and Emily arguing. Emily said, "Have you lost your mind?"

They couldn't hear what Harry answered.

Ruthie said, "Daddy, you look the same. We missed you, but Mama took good care of us."

"She taught us how to dig clams and she let us wade in the water at Huff's Neck. Maybe you can get the house we had in the old neighborhood and the three of us can live there."

Tom stopped walking, crouched his six-foot frame down and said, "Girls, let's not try to rush things. Wherever I wind up living, it will be close to you from now on."

"We're going to introduce you to a new friend just a couple of houses from here, is that okay?"

"I guess so."

"She is Mim Nichol. She is our friend. We had to sneak to her house at first, but now it's okay."

"Why did you sneak?"

"Emily didn't want us to become friends with the neighbors. When they said Mama died, Mim came to our house so now it's okay to go to hers."

Mim had seen them come up the walk and was waiting in her door way. "Hi, girls, who do we have here?"

She studied the six-foot Tom with his blonde hair and very light blue eyes and added, "I bet this is your Daddy. He has your coloring. Come in, come in."

The three of them entered Mim's living room and smelled the familiar smell of something delicious baking.

"I just baked some cookies. Let's sit down and talk about your plans if you have some. We'll have the cookies, too."

Mim left the living room and brought a plate of cookies still warm from the oven.

Ruthie said, "This is our Daddy. He came back like our Mama said he would. We want to live with him. Do you think you can find a place for the three of us?"

Tom said, "It's nice to meet you, thank you for being a friend to my daughters. They think so much of you they might be rushing into things."

"I understand."

She turned to Ruthie, "Gosh, I don't know of a place right now. But once your Daddy is settled, maybe we can talk about it then. Help yourselves to the cookies."

Beth said, "Mim, did they make a mistake about our mother? Shouldn't we go to the funeral home so we can see?"

"Listen, dear, it's not likely there was a mistake made. So many people are involved every one of them couldn't have been wrong, does that make sense? I don't know about the funeral home visit. Maybe Emily wants you to remember her the way she was. I think she mentioned that to me."

Tom said, "Thank you for that, Mim and for the cookies. We better be leaving. I am taking them to Brigham's for a sundae."

Mim stood and said, "You're all very welcome and come any time."

As the three left Mim's house, Ruthie said, "Isn't she nice?"

"She really is. An idea came to me as we visited her. I have a friend I can live with right here in Quincy. She owns an antique shop, and she is a lot like Mim. I feel certain you can visit anytime."

Ruthie asked, "Can we go with you?"

"I wouldn't want to make that promise."

Chapter 22

After Tom, Ruthie and Beth left Mim's house, they walked along under the huge red maple trees now in full fall color. Some of the leaves had fallen forming piles of brown crunchy curls next to the curbs. Ruthie and Beth liked to crush them, but today they refrained choosing instead to pay more attention to their Dad.

Ruthie said, "You are going to the funeral, aren't you? Can you take us?"

"Yes, I'll be there, but I have to respect what Emily wants so I won't be able to take you with me. That doesn't mean I agree with her on this. She won't give an inch on it, and if I take you it could cause her to take it out on both of you." He held up Ruthie's thick blonde braids and let them bounce on her back.

"That's not fair, she's our mother and we want to see her again," Beth added.

"Girls, try to remember all the good times like when she took you to the beach and dug clams. And how well she took care of you. Emily makes mistakes but she is probably right about both of you trying to remember her alive and happy with you. Look, here we are at Brigham's."

Ruthie made a note in her mind to ask Tom about Emily's mistakes. She felt justified about her feelings knowing that her own father knew Emily had made mistakes. Could it be committing her to the hospital at Medfield was one of them? She thought her father sounded as if he missed their mother as much as they did.

The three entered the ice cream store where a girl was at the front window dipping peppermints, the familiar smell of melting chocolate was all over the place. A small crowd had gathered to watch outside. Ruthie stopped too see her dip and drain the newly made candies. She quickly joined Beth and Tom already in the booth they had chosen near the middle of the store.

They were talking about what to order, plain dishes of ice cream or sundaes like they had planned. When Ruthie sat down, all three decided on the sundaes with everything on them.

Most of the time they opted for just the hot fudge.

Ruthie said, "In celebration of Daddy coming home, let's have nuts, cherries and marshmallow.

Tom and Beth nodded agreement.

Beth said, "We never get the cherries. But today we will just for you." She snuggled close to Tom in the booth.

Tom laughed and reached to squeeze their sun tanned hands. "Thank you for this."

Ruthie wondered if Tom would stay close by. She was slightly frightened he might go away again. Then she thought of Mim. They'd still have her. Her mother said Tom would come back. Did she mean he would come back to stay?

"Is Mrs. Alexander going to let us come to see you? Can you show us where she lives on Hancock Street?" Ruthie asked.

The waitress came with the sundaes. After she left the area, Tom said, "As soon as we finish here we can walk to where I'll be staying. It's close."

"Gee, did you already tell her about us, and fix it so you can stay there?" Ruthie asked.

"Sort of. I told her I was going to be in Quincy where my daughters are. She asked me where I was staying. When I told her I was unsure, she offered me to stay with her as long as I want."

Beth said, "Wow, she must be a great friend."

"Have you had her for a friend for a long time?" Ruthie asked

"Years ago I helped her fix and refinish furniture. I'll be working for her, again. Fixing antiques and helping her to move those she sells."

They ate in silence. Each enjoying every spoonful, until Ruthie said, "You know I think the next time I'll just have the hot fudge. All this other goo is too much to eat."

Tom said, "Okay, let's pay for this stuff, and go to the antique shop."

Beth and Ruthie hurried to the front of the store to watch the girl dipping the chocolates. The clerk saw them and said, "Want to try one?"

Beth said, "Yes, we would." Then to Ruthie, "Wouldn't we?"

"Oh, yes they look good. Can we have one for our Dad?"

"Of course." She handed three samples to Ruthie.

Tom approached just in time to get his, and tell the girls they had better be on their way.

Ruthie and Beth thanked the clerk for the samples.

The traffic was slightly heavy so Tom advised them to stay together as they crossed the wide street. On the other side, he said, "It's just three blocks down on this side."

Ruthie said, "This is great, Daddy, it's close to Emily's house. We can see you all the time."

Ruthie was still confused over why Tom couldn't have the back bedroom upstairs in Emily's house. She realized then it wouldn't work, and there would be arguing all the time, because it seemed Emily didn't like him even though he was her father, too.

"That's what I want," Tom said.

"I wonder if Emily will be mad at us," Beth added.

Ruthie became upset. "Who cares? I'll sneak if I have to."

"That's not a good thing, Ruthie," Tom said. "We'll find a way so you don't have to do that."

They came to a white house with green shutters and a sign hanging over the porch, "Alexander's Antiques."

"Is this it? Is this where you will live, Daddy?"

"This is it."

Ruthie and Beth stood close as their Dad entered the store.

Beth whispered to Ruthie, "What if we don't like her?"

"We will. I can feel it."

Then a small woman dressed in light green with brown hair clipped back with a black barrette came out on the porch. Some stray hairs stuck out of the barrette, but she was neat like Ruthie's mother.

Ruthie heard her say, "Tom, how nice." She hugged him. "I'm so glad you are here, are these your daughters?"

Tom motioned for Ruthie and Beth to come on the porch. Ruthie wondered about the hug this woman gave to her father. She consoled herself thinking how stupid, friends hug each other.

Tom said, "Ruthie and Beth, I'd like you to meet my good friend, Margaret Alexander. Mrs. Alexander to you."

They both said meekly, "Hello."

She said, "Let's go through the store, and I'll show you where your Daddy will live if he wants."

They entered a large room with tables, chairs, mirrors and other furniture neatly placed with tags on them. Ruthie wondered if anyone actually bought any of these things because they had scratches on them, like Mr. Barney's old piano.

The four of them squeezed by some of the things that hadn't been put on display, Mrs. Alexander led the way. Beth nudged Ruthie and said, "She's nice."

"Yes, she is."

The next room they entered was a bright kitchen with a canary in a cage in the corner. It fluttered and moved down from its perch.

"Don't worry, she'll get used to new people around. Her name is Betsy."

Ruthie looked around the warm kitchen with a teapot on the stove like Mrs. McKinnel had. "We stayed with a friend who had a kitchen like this. It was a happy time."

"I hope you have those happy times here. You are welcome anytime."

Beth remained quiet like she was still not sure, then she blurted out, "Are you going to marry my Daddy?"

Ruthie looked at the startled look on the faces of Tom and Mrs. Alexander and thought with sadness, "No chance of the three of us living together, unless the four of us could. Why couldn't the four of us live here? We don't have to call her mother or mama, she'll be a friend."

Chapter 23

After the visit to Mrs. Alexander's shop, Beth and Ruthie kissed Tom goodbye before they left to go back to Emily's house. Home.

Ruthie lingered and then asked, "Will you tell us all about the funeral?" She squeezed his hand and clung to his waist and added, "You aren't going away again, are you?"

"Hey, Hey, everything is going to be alright. We'll see each other whenever we want from now on. I'm staying with Mrs. Alexander, remember?"

Beth threw herself at Tom and clung just as Ruthie did.

Tom continued, "What is all this? We're together at last and yes I'll tell you all about the funeral. I love you, now scoot, Emily will be looking for you. I'm not going anywhere."

They said goodbye to Mrs. Alexander, Betsey the canary and left through the shop.

When they reached the street, Ruthie said, "Shall we sneak to the funeral home? It's right down the street from here." She wanted to make sure it was her mother, but she really didn't want to know for sure her mother was dead. Though mixed up on her feelings, she decided to find out.

"Yeah, let's do it," Beth said. Ruthie couldn't rely on this, because Beth went along with whatever made sense at any given time. But, in her own mind she had to know if it was her mother.

They headed along Hancock Street. A slight autumn breeze blew. They crunched fallen leaves as they walked.

Beth said, "What if it isn't Mama? What if it is? What will we do?"

"We have to make a plan," Ruthie explained, remembering a suggestion by her mother long ago.

"We go into the funeral home and try to find where Mama is. When we see her, if we do, we look at her good. If it's her, remember we can't cry or yell or anything like that, because they might call Emily. Can you do that?"

"If you can, I can." Ruthie wasn't sure she could count on that.

She said, "Here we are, remember the plan." They walked up the steps onto a large porch and opened a glass door that read Russell

Brothers Funeral Home in gold letters. A fountain bubbled near the porch, but everything else was quiet.

"Wow, is this for dead people?" Beth said looking at all the soft couches and chairs.

"Let me do the talking."

Inside a young man dressed in a black suit approached them, "May I help you young ladies?"

"Yes, we came to see Joan Brooks? Our mother."

"Is anyone else with you? How old are you?" the man asked.

Ruthie said, "No, we came by ourselves. I am thirteen, and my sister here is nine. Please let us see our mother; we want to say good-bye. I know she can't hear us, but please."

Beth folded her hands as tight as she could and kept quiet, as Ruthie had told her.

Surprisingly the man agreed and said, "I probably shouldn't do this, but follow me." The man had gray curly hair that looked soft. His voice was gentle. He was so kind, Ruthie felt sure he loved their mother as much as she and Beth.

Ruthie clutched Beth and said, "Wow, can you believe it?"

They entered another room on the side of the big house. The man directed them to a large dark wood shiny box. Bouquets of flowers were nearby. One was a red rose with a white ribbon that read "Mother."

Helen was lying in there dressed in blue with her head resting on a white pillow. Her hair was twisted into the same soft bun.

She looked like she was alive, but asleep.

Ruthie grabbed Beth and they rushed toward the casket.

"Mama, mama it is you," Ruthie said flinging herself on Helen's chest.

Beth stood back and saw her mother didn't move, "No, I'm leaving, I'm afraid," she said and began to cry.

The young man who had given them permission to see Helen, softly said, "Girls, just say good bye like you told me. Then you have to go." He gently moved Ruthie away from the casket.

Ruthie made herself stop crying and said, "Bye, Mama, we love you. You'll always be our mother."

Beth changed her mind and came near to add, "When we go to the beach, we'll dig clams just for you." She threw Helen a kiss.

The man led them to the same door they had come in. "Girls, I am so sorry. You look nice, and I know your mother would be proud."

They walked down the steps and stood on the sidewalk. Ruthie said, "It is her. She looked beautiful, but they forgot her powder. I couldn't smell it."

Beth said, "Maybe they don't put powder on dead people. We have no mother. Just Mim. She looked like she was asleep. She wasn't, because she didn't answer us, she is dead," Beth said.

Ruthie admonished Beth, "You can't tell anyone about this, except maybe Mim. Don't even tell Daddy or especially Emily."

"I won't."

"You always say that, but sometimes you do tell things. This is important, Beth, you can't tell. We'll all get in trouble, even that nice man who let us in. We better be getting home."

Beth said, "Can we go to Mac's and get some of those potato chips and an orange drink?"

Ruthie really didn't feel like eating anything, even Mac's treats, she said, "I guess so, but we have to hurry so Emily won't get mad. Don't let her know we got money from Daddy." Mac's potato chips were the best. He kept them in a square glass container and scooped them out with a large scoop. The bags he used seemed very small. Nobody ever got enough for the money.

They hurried along Elm Avenue towards his variety store.

Ruthie said, "I have another plan. If it isn't too late when we get home, we'll go to Mim's and tell her everything. About Mrs. Alexander, the sneaking to the funeral home and Mac's okay?"

"Yeah, Mim will make us feel better. Let's pretend she is our mother."

"No, we told Mama she'd always be our mother."

Chapter 24

When Beth and Ruthie left Mac's, they walked along the chain link fence surrounding Massie, Beth's school. Beth said, "Gee, we have to go to school tomorrow. I hope the kids don't mention Mama."

"Most likely they will. All you have to say is something like, "It was sad, and we cried, but our Dad is with us.'"

"Gee that's a good thing to say. Do we have time to go to Mim's?"

"If we hurry."

"Are we going to tell her everything?"

"I guess so. She can tell us what we should do next. Maybe she can think of a plan to have you, me and Daddy live together." Ruthie wondered is it possible the three of us could move in with Mim? She has such a big house. No, that wouldn't work; it's too close to Emily.

"I thought we gave that up because of Mrs. Alexander."

"Mrs. Alexander is just a friend. She doesn't own Daddy. He likes her, she helps him, and he works on her antiques."

"Don't forget, we can't stay long." Ruthie made sure they came down the side of Mim's house furthest from Emily's in case Emily was watching for them."

They went up the stairs where Mim was waiting with her arms open. "I saw you two coming up the street, and I hoped you were coming to see me."

Ruthie and Beth rushed into Mim who hugged them, warmly. She was dressed in her familiar navy blue dress and slippers. She usually wore slippers.

Ruthie began to cry and shortly after she began, Beth cried, too. Ruthie wasn't really sad, because she always loved to visit Mim. For some unknown reason the warm reception made her cry.

"Hey, hey, what's the matter? Come in and sit on your little couch and we can talk."

They stopped crying and followed her into her living room towards the same little couch where they usually sat. It felt like home the way Mim had said "your little couch."

Ruthie said, "It's always so nice here, thank you, Mim."

Impulsive Beth said, "We sneaked to the funeral home. It was Ruthie's idea, and a man let us see Mama, dead. She looked like she was asleep. Ruthie flopped on top of her, and then she said she couldn't smell her powder."

Turning to Ruthie, Mim asked, "Is this true? My goodness, you were fortunate the man let you see her. How do you feel now?"

"Yes, it is true, but please don't tell anyone. Well, now we know the hospital didn't make a mistake. She looked soft and nice, but asleep. I couldn't feel her warmth. Do you think we are awful?"

Ruthie watched Mim's tiny smile as she shook her head, approvingly.

"First of all, No, I don't think you are awful, and what is more, I think your mother would support you. Secondly, be careful not to tell anyone, because it may upset Emily. If that happens, the man who allowed it could get into trouble. So let's keep it here."

"Okay, we will, won't we, Beth?" Ruthie thought she could trust Beth on this.

"Yes."

"Did you get your sundaes with your father?"

Ruthie said, "Yup, we did, and it worked out good. He took us to Mrs. Alexander's Antique Shop where he will be living and working. She seems nice and invited us to come anytime we want."

"I asked if she was going to marry my daddy, but she didn't tell us," Beth said.

Mim laughed and winked at Beth. "I wouldn't want to comment one way or the other."

Ruthie didn't waste any time in approaching the bigger question. "Mim, do you think we could find a way to live with our father? It would be the three of us. Can you help us? Can you think of a way?"

"Slow down, dear. Let's think of what you are asking. I would be involving myself into Emily and Charlotte's business. I am not sure that would be right or if it would even work."

"Why? They like you. I know they do."

Beth added, "We would still come and see you."

Mim laughed again, pushed that same stray hair from her face and said, "I'm not worried about that, really. I just don't want you two to get into any unpleasant situations with your sisters."

Beth said, "We don't care about them, only you and Daddy, isn't that right Ruthie?"

"She's right, Mim. Just you and Daddy."

She rushed towards Mim and dropped into her lap with Beth close behind.

"I'll tell you what I'll do," Mim said, patting both of them.

They sat up on their knees in front of her chair. Ruthie said, "I knew you'd have an idea."

"That's right, Mim, she told me you would help," added Beth.

"I'll find a way to talk to Charlotte and Emily. But not right away, because of the funeral, and the fact that they probably don't want to discuss anything this serious right now. Does that make sense?"

"Yes, we'll wait. Now we have to go before we get into trouble with Emily. She didn't want us to go to Brigham's. Harry said we could."

Mim's face brightened as she said, "Gee, that's good news. Maybe Harry will be your friend."

Devil may care Beth said, "No, he's not. He doesn't want Emily to get mad at him. He's always lovey around her. Maybe he wanted to get us out of the house when he made her let us go with Daddy."

"Now, Beth, give him a chance. He hasn't been home from the Navy very long and maybe he is trying to readjust himself."

"Oh, okay, I'll try. But if they ever separate Ruthie and me, again, we'll run away. Wont, we Ruthie?"

"Fast. We really have to go, Beth." Ruthie said as she hugged Mim around the waist.

Beth grabbed her hand and squeezed it as they both headed to the front door.

Ruthie called over her shoulder, "Don't forget to think of a plan so we can live with Daddy."

"I'll try to talk to Charlotte and Emily as soon as the time is right."

When they reached the bottom step of the porch, Ruthie told Beth, "The time will never be right. You watch."

Chapter 25

As Beth and Ruthie walked toward Emily's house, Ruthie said, "Remember not to let anything slip about seeing Mama. Emily will be very angry and maybe even blame Daddy."

"Okay, I'll be careful."

"Now, Beth, this time I mean it. Too many people will get hurt."

"Okay, okay, I won't say anything."

They walked down the gravel driveway to the back door. Ruthie said, "Look the Marigolds are still blooming. Mama loved Marigolds. Maybe we can pick some and have Emily take them to the funeral home"

"You can ask her. I'm not."

Emily was in the kitchen ironing. She looked up and said, "Well, I take it you had a wonderful time with your so called father."

Ruthie felt a little queasy hearing the accusation. She only said, "We went to Brigham's and had the sundaes. They were good, but we wanted more hot fudge. It seems like they never give enough."

"You've been gone a long time."

Before Ruthie could answer, Beth, added, "Yeah, and after that we went to Mrs. Alexander's house, where Daddy will be living."

Ruthie shot her a look as if to signal not to say any more.

Emily said, "You, what? Went where? Ruthie you better tell me. Harry, come out here. You started this."

Ruthie said, "No it wasn't anything bad." She cried.

Harry came into the kitchen and said, "Now, what's going on?"

Before Ruthie could explain anything, Emily quickly responded, "You let these two go off with their father, and he took them to his girl friend's house."

Ruthie glanced at Beth kept quiet. She was grateful.

"It wasn't like that, honest." Ruthie said as she crossed the kitchen and clutched Harry's hand.

He said, "Calm down. Emily that's not fair. Let them tell where they went and what happened."

Ruthie smiled a little inside smile because it seemed like Harry was going to stand by them, after all. She said, "We went to the antique store that Daddy's friend owns. Her name is Mrs. Alexander, and because Daddy doesn't have a place to live, she said he could live there in return for helping her with the antiques."

"Oh, that's great. See, Harry, I told you they shouldn't go with that wretch."

Beth lunged at Emily and screamed, "He's not a wretch, and you are."

Emily slapped her hard on the arm. "Don't you dare talk to me that way. Go to your room right now." Beth left the kitchen, Ruthie felt sorry she was crying but thought. What will I do now? I'll have to get out of this the best way I can. I'll get Beth later, she started it.

Ruthie explained, "The lady is nice and was trying to help Daddy. She said we could visit her anytime we wanted. She said she has known him for a long time, and that they were friends. Not girl friend boyfriend, but regular friends."

Harry intervened again, "Emily give them a chance. We couldn't take him in. Maybe this is a good thing. We don't even know this woman. It's just unfair to make any accusations. And, it's too early." Then to Ruthie who still clung to him he said, "It's okay, go up with Beth. We'll get this straightened out."

Ruthie squeezed his hand and left the kitchen.

When she entered her room, Beth was lying on the bed. "Look what's happening now because of you and your big mouth. I told you not to say anything."

"No, you did not. You said the funeral home. I didn't say anything about the funeral home, did I?"

"Do I have to tell you every little thing not to say? Just be quiet about all this stuff, will you?"

"Okay, but don't be mad. I'll try harder."

Emily came into the bedroom. "What's this about the funeral home? Did your father take you there after I told him not to?"

Beth answered before Ruthie. "No, we asked him, but he said we had to respect your wishes."

Ruthie was relieved Beth didn't mention that he had said Emily had made mistakes.

She changed the subject. "Emily is it okay if we pick some of your Marigolds for a bouquet and you can take them to funeral home? Mama loved them."

"I guess that will be alright. You get them ready, and I'll take them tomorrow for the funeral."

She turned to Beth. "Now, young lady, don't you ever talk back to me again."

Just above a whisper, Beth said, "I won't."

Emily went downstairs.

Once she was out of earshot, Ruthie said, "If we didn't have to go to school, we could sneak to watch the funeral."

"Could we play hookey?"

"I might, but you're not, you talk too much."

Chapter 26

The next morning Ruthie woke up earlier than usual. Today was the day of her mother's funeral. She thought about her mother lying on the white pillow in her blue dress. She was still there. She might be dead, but she was still in the world. Later she would be in the ground in the cemetery. She'd never see her again in the hospital, at the beach or even at the funeral home. Her mother wouldn't want her to be sad.

She went to the closet, in silence, not disturbing Beth, to pick out her clothes for the day.

What if she skipped school? Maybe she could get Mary Ann to skip with her and they could sneak to the funeral. Mary Ann usually could be convinced, but maybe not because skipping school was serious. They could get in trouble at school and then again at home. Emily would go wild. Mary Ann's parents were softer.

She decided against it and rifled through her clothes. She picked out a navy blue skirt and a short sleeved white shirt. After she dressed, she brushed her thick hair and let it hang loose over her shoulders. Emily always wanted it tied back, but Ruthie thought she might not notice because of the sadness of the funeral.

Ruthie went downstairs into the kitchen. Emily was there looking pale and sickly in her navy blue robe. She should look sickly after what she did to mama and Beth and me, thought Ruthie. She'll probably really be sick at the funeral.

She said, "Hi Emily, Beth is still in bed. Shall I get her up?"

"I guess you better."

Ruthie yelled from the bottom of the stairs, "Hey, Beth, Emily said it's time to get up."

"Okay, I'm coming."

Emily said, "Usually families stay together during the loss of a mother. Harry and I decided that it would be better for you to go on to school with your friends."

"I'd like to go to the funeral." Ruthie had already seen her mother so she wasn't very forceful in expressing herself. Emily didn't notice.

"Let's not get into that again. Eat your breakfast, and then go get Mary Ann so you can walk to school. Time is getting short."

Short for who? Ruthie wondered. You never thought about it being short or long when mama tried to get food for us in Huff's Neck. Short for you, maybe, long for us.

Ruthie sat down and began to pick at the bowl of cereal. It was always the same, thick lumpy oatmeal with brown sugar and milk. Today was no different.

Beth came into the kitchen and headed to the table. "Yuck, not this stuff again."

Emily was in her bedroom so she didn't hear. Ruthie kicked Beth under the table.

Beth said, "Hey, Ruthie are you going to sneak? You know remember how you said you might sneak? We could do it like we did at the funeral home."

"We? Shut up. Even if I decide I'm not telling you."

They finished in silence.

Ruthie took the dishes to the sink and said, "Bye Emily. Bye Beth."

Beth said, "Yeah, bye. See you after school. I guess you are going to school."

Ruthie squinted her eyes in a glare at Beth.

Emily came back to the kitchen with lunch money for both of them.

She said, "Come right home after school."

"Okay," Ruthie said as she went out the back door.

Mary Ann was waiting in her usual spot under the big tree in front of their house. The morning was bright a soft autumn breeze blew. Mary Ann had her dark hair hanging loose over her red sweater that matched a pleated plaid skirt.

Mary Ann said, "Hi. I wasn't sure you'd be coming to school today."

"Oh, yeah, I wanted to go to the funeral. Emily said no."

"She's probably right for once. It would be too sad."

"Yeah, I suppose so, but Beth and I wanted to go. I have some good news; my father is back. Beth and I want to live with him. Emily is against it. She despises our father. I'm not sure he's so crazy about her."

"Gee, if that does happen, I hope you won't have to move far away."

"It's not going to happen. We have Mim trying to work on that, too, but I don't think it will happen. Anyway we won't move, because he is living near. Do you think kids will say anything about my mother?"

"Some might, but they won't be mean."

"Yeah, people say what they think you want to hear, don't they?"

"A lot of the time"

They arrived at the school, Mary Ann said, "See you at lunch."

"Okay, lunch." Ruthie decided. She thought she'd give up everything to see mama one last time. What if mama wanted us to be there? Emily doesn't know everything. What if she's wrong? Maybe Beth is as sad as I am and covered it up.

Just then Patti Kolbeck came walking towards her. She quickly wiped a smile off of her face and said, "Hi Ruthie. I'm sorry about your mother."

Ruthie felt embarrassed, and put her head down slightly, not wanting anyone to feel sorry for her but she said," Thanks." To herself she said here it goes. She wondered if she was sorry. She has her mother who probably told her to say at least that. Most kids said the stuff they were told to say. She has no way to know what it's like to be without a mother. Ruthie hurried the other way through the crowded hall. That's when she spied the notice on the main bulletin board: Cheerleading tryouts this afternoon at 2:30 in the gym.

Her mind raced back to her own mother on the white pillow. She heard her whisper, "Always have a plan."

Ruthie said softly to herself. I have a plan Mama, I'm going out for cheerleading this afternoon. I didn't sneak to the funeral, because I wasn't sure you would want that. Daddy did come back. Maybe Beth and I can live with him.

Chapter 27

Ruthie struggled to get through the day. She kept thinking about the funeral and watching the clock. Each time she looked at the clock she wondered if her mother was still in the world not in the ground. She was bolstered by the fact her mother wouldn't want her to be sad.

In Miss Waddell's English class, Miss Waddell called on her to read. She stood in the isle beside her desk and began to read some paragraphs from Ivanhoe. She made herself take interest. It was when Miss Waddell said, "Very good, Ruthie," that Ruthie realized she was pushing on.

But, she kept seeing her mother on the white pillow. Not moving. Her mother would never move again. She was gone for good. Maybe Daddy will take them to live with him when he realizes they were so alone. She decided to make that her goal.

When the bell rang to go to the last class, Miss Waddell beckoned to Ruthie. Ruthie walked towards her desk and said, "Did I do something wrong?"

"No, I just wanted you to be aware of the cheerleading tryouts this afternoon. Remember we talked about them and that you would be the perfect mascot?"

"Yes, and I saw the notice on the bulletin board in the hall. I'm planning to be there right after school gets out."

"Good. That's what I wanted to hear. You're going to be fine, Ruthie. I feel it, and you will make your mother proud." She squeezed her hand and added, "You may go, now. See you tomorrow."

Ruthie smiled. "I'll let you know how it went."

Ruthie rushed from the class to her civics class. She asked herself if this day would end happily or would she get into a mess of trouble with Emily for not going right home from school.

She tried to pay attention in the civics lesson, but most of it was a blur. She didn't care about the pyramids in Egypt.

The bell rang at 2:30. Ruthie grabbed her homework and hurried into the noisy hall traffic.

She felt a tug at her sleeve. Joan Crosby, a friend from another class said, "Hi, Ruthie. I'm sorry about your mother, but you are going to cheerleading tryouts aren't you?"

"Yeah, it's weird, but I think my mother would want me there, so I am going. I hope people don't think I'm awful for doing that."

"No," Joan said, "They'll feel like I do, that you're brave."

They walked together toward the gym where Mary Ann was waiting.

She said, "Hi, Ruthie, I'm glad you're here. I'm so excited for you, I know you'll get picked."

Ruthie put her books down near Mary Ann's stuff and said, "I hope you're right. It might help me to worry about other things instead of not having my mother anymore."

Miss Cash, the person in charge of choosing called for everyone's attention. "Will the candidates line up over here? Just form a straight line down the middle of the gym. Ten cheerleaders will be picked today. I decided to do it that way so you wouldn't be nervous wrecks over night."

A wave of pokes and whispers went through the crowd of candidates. Around twenty-five girls walked to the center of the floor and formed the line. Ruthie thought if she were picked from all those girls, it would be a miracle.

"That's good," continued Miss Cash. "Now march around the gym. Last years cheerleaders will teach you what to do in groups."

Small groups were formed and short cheers were taught. A girl named Libby handed each in Ruthie's group a small sheet with a cheer typed on it. She gave them time to study it. Ruthie's read: Central rah, are we in it? Yes we are. Who, what, when, where? Central High right in there.

It was an easy rhyme. Ruthie memorized it, and Libby called on each one to take a turn. When it was Ruthie's turn, she did so well without the paper, the other kids clapped.

After each one had a turn, Miss Cash called them back to the side near the bleachers.

She explained that each would cheer in front of the rest of the candidates.

The eliminations would take place as each took a turn. We will begin alphabetically. So Ruthie was first.

She walked forward, stood tall, moved her arms as instructed by Libby and recited the cheer.

Some of the other candidates clapped as she took her seat on the bleachers.

At the end of the tryouts, Miss Cash read the names of those picked. Mary Ann and Ruthie made the team. Some of the girls not chosen could be heard sniffling.

Miss Cash said, "May I have your attention once more. The new candidates meet here tomorrow for the first practice and information about the uniforms."

Ruthie and Mary Ann were so excited. On the way home they talked about going to the games, wearing their uniforms to school and getting out of school early on game days.

As they neared their street, Ruthie said, "Oh, gee, Mary Ann, I am so late getting home, Emily will be furious."

"What else is new? She's always furious even when you do what's right."

"I guess I'll just tell her the truth. Let her rip into me. I might as well get it over with."

"Hey, that's great! Maybe she'll give in, and be happy for you. Maybe you won't have to go to Mim Nicol or Miss Waddell for help with the uniform. What if she decides to get it for you? And, don't forget there is always Harry. He could help."

"Yeah, it's possible. I feel sure they won't make me resign. I think I'll offer to do extra work around the house to earn the money for the uniform. Gee, I just remembered, maybe my father will get it for me. I know Emily would be upset if she knew a teacher or Mim Nicol was going to help. Thanks, Mary Ann. This is going to work."

"Okay, I'll see you tomorrow."

"Okay, bye."

On the way down the driveway, Ruthie became nervous again. She thought all the stuff she and Mary Ann had mentioned might never work. She had heard someone call that talk lip service. Emily would be

jealous because she was never more than a Brownie. She walked slowly

up the back steps to the kitchen.

Chapter 28

Ruthie reached the kitchen still thinking about Emily being a Brownie and probably yelling and screaming at the other Brownies, but suddenly she felt dizzy when she walked in the middle of Emily, Harry and Beth. Emily and Harry were still dressed in the clothes they wore to the funeral. She thought here it goes the mess with Emily that Marianne and I had figured. Beth had distanced herself by standing in the pantry doorway, but when she saw Ruthie, she grimaced.

Emily said, "Okay, Miss Priss, where have you been this time? I thought you were so upset about the funeral. You were so set on going. You couldn't have been too intent on going or you would have come home right away to find out what happened. Look at you; you're a mess. I asked you not to let your hair hang loose.".

Ruthie hung her head and began to cry. Her hair had become sweaty and straggly from the tryouts. "I did want to go. You wouldn't let me. I was afraid all the kids would say stuff, but you never even thought about that. All you said was I'd be better off with my friends."

"I thought I was protecting you from extra sadness, you little ingrate. That's the reason I didn't want you to go. Harry and I talked it over, and we thought it was best you went on to school. I can see we were right, because you took your time coming home, even after I had told you to come right home."

Ruthie wiped her eyes with the back of her hand and sniffed. She said, "Emily, you act like you're the only one who loved Mama. If you really loved her, why didn't you ever come to see her? She used to tell Beth and me you would come. She said, 'Charlotte and Emily will come for us. That never happened until the day after they took her away and then you kept us waiting another whole day at the Mckinnels. Then she died in that awful hospital. Well today I did what I knew Mama would have wanted. There were cheerleading tryouts. I went to the gym at three o'clock, tried out and was picked."

Emily rushed across the kitchen, grabbed Ruthie by the front of her shirt and screamed, "How dare you, you brat. You can just go back tomorrow and tell them you are not allowed to be a part of the squad."

Beth cried and said, "That's mean. Just because you only made the Brownies."

Emily turned on Beth and screamed, "You stay out of this."

Harry stepped into the tussle saying, "Hold on, hold it. Emily stop it. She's not quitting anything. Give them a break. They have been through a lot. You were the one who said they couldn't go to the funeral. So, they did what you wanted and you're still not satisfied."

Ruthie had wondered whose idea it was. She was right Harry would have let them go. It was Emily again. She had to get away and live with her father. She was sure about one thing, she would tell her father how awful Emily was acting now.

Then Harry turned to Ruthie and said, "I think it's nice you were chosen, and something else, too, I think your mother would be happy that you are trying to lead a life like other kids."

Emily said, "Oh, thanks a lot." Her voice trailed off.

Harry announced, "Emily, you've said enough. Try to be happy for her." He left the kitchen.

Ruthie and Beth took their books and homework and headed upstairs to their bedroom.

On the way up the stairs, Beth said, "Gee, Ruthie, that is great! I can go to the games and tell all the kids you're my sister."

Ruthie laughed. "It's not that big a deal. But I am excited. Gee, Beth I couldn't believe you mentioned the Brownies to Emily. I was glad, but we'll hear more about that. Wait until Harry goes back to the Navy. I have a feeling we're in for it."

"When is he going back anyway? I'm not scared. I'll leave and go live with Daddy at Mrs. Alexander's house. Can you picture the old witch in the little brown dress? I bet she didn't have any badges. She probably tried to take over the meetings from the leader."

Ruthie said, "Beth, stop it, you sound like Emily. I think Harry leaves in two weeks. I'd like to go to Mim and tell her about the cheerleading. I have to find a way to get the money for the uniform. Mim said she would help, but maybe Harry would do it."

"You better not mention anymore about it today, and that includes trying to get to Mim's house."

"Oh, yeah? Watch me. When I empty the trash tonight after supper, I'm sneaking down to Mim's house."

Chapter 29

Around five o'clock when Beth and Ruthie were still upstairs in their bedroom doing homework, after the confrontation with Emily, Emily called, "Ruthie, Beth, set the table for supper."

Ruthie said, "We're coming."

She turned to Beth and said, "She still sounds upset."

"Yeah, well don't start it up again. And don't sneak to Mim's when you empty the trash. That will get it going for sure."

"Mind your business."

They headed to the kitchen. It smelled like Emily was cooking spaghetti again, the only thing she cooked that was any good.

Beth whispered, "Spaghetti. It's all she does." Beth put the silver around the table, and Ruthie set the dishes in the middle of each setting. A red-checkered tablecloth was on the table. The settings were close together, because the table was pushed against the wall below two windows making it a little difficult to maneuver around that side. Beth and Ruthie had to be careful not to change anything, because the kitchen was always neat. The café style curtains always looked as though they had just been washed and ironed. Nothing ever changed.

Emily said, "Don't forget the napkins." She tossed five napkins on the table.

Beth said, "We won't, and we won't forget the rolls and butter."

Emily turned on her and shouted, "You're getting a little big for your britches, aren't you?"

Beth hung her head and said, "Sorry." Ruthie was worried Emily would say something about the way Beth had apologized. Ruthie knew she wasn't the least bit sorry, and she made it sound like it.

"You better be."

There was very little conversation during the supper. Ruthie liked having spaghetti, because it was the one meal Emily managed to serve hot. She usually had good bread or rolls, too.

Beth did ask, "Harry, when do you have to back to the Navy? We'll miss you."

"Well, Beth that's nice. I leave in two weeks. After that, I'm not sure when I'll be home again. It may be awhile."

Ruthie asked, "Where will you go? Do you go on a ship?"

"Yes, I go on a destroyer. It's small compared to a battleship or aircraft carrier. But once you get used to living with a bunch of guys and having your own small space, it's okay. I wouldn't want to do it all the time, though."

Emily said, "We have Jello for desert."

Ruthie thought not again. She doesn't know how to make anything different. She remembered her mother taking free fish from Jake the fisherman and sharing one potato between the three of them. Everything tasted good. They couldn't afford Jello. She thought about Emily eating everything while they were hungry most of the time.

Ruthie said, "Good, I'll clear the table and get the dessert dishes."

"If you think that will put you on my good side, you're sadly mistaken."

"I wasn't trying to do that," Ruthie said. "I was trying to help."

Harry glared at Emily, who quickly stopped.

Beth said, "Emily, when you have your good side, it never lasts very long. It seems like you are nice and then you get mad all over again. Don't you want us here?"

Ruthie knew this was Beth's way of getting the opportunity to leave and live with their father at Mrs. Alexander's house.

Emily said, "If you girls would cooperate more, maybe I would show my good side more. It has nothing to do with wanting you here at all; of course I want you here. Harry does, too."

Harry said, "Let's drop this, before it gets too involved." Ruthie brought the Jello.

Beth said, "I don't want any, I hate Jello, especially lemon Jello. Jello after spaghetti, yuck."

Harry said, "You're excused, Beth."

Beth hurried upstairs to the bedroom.

Ruthie ate the Jello in silence and when the meal was over, cleared the table.

She said, "Shall I get Beth to help with the dishes?"

Harry said, "Yes, that's a good idea." He called Beth who came to the kitchen right away.

He said, "Beth that was rude remark you made about the Jello. No thank you would have been enough."

She looked at him and said, "I'm really sorry. I won't do it anymore."

"That's better. Now help with the dishes."

Harry and Emily went into to the living room. Ruthie heard a low conversation, but couldn't hear what was said. It was mostly

Emily doing the talking, so Ruthie figured it was about she and Beth.

Ruthie asked Beth, "Do you want to wash or dry?"

"I'll wash. I don't like either one."

After they finished and put everything away, Ruthie said, "I guess I'll empty the trash."

Beth said, "I'll go with you."

Ruthie agreed to avoid a quarrel with her. She didn't care if they both sneaked to Mim's, because Beth knew the reason for the visit anyway. Beth told things more than Ruthie liked, but she decided to take a chance that night.

Ruthie took the wastebasket. "Beth, you can at least carry the garbage." The garbage was in a white enamel pan.

They quietly crept down the back stairway to the barrels and the garbage can. It was nearly dark, but there was enough light from the kitchen window so they could find their way.

Beth said, "Are we going to sneak? It's getting a little late."

"Yes, but be quiet and don't tell anything when we get back. Just say we walked up the street."

"In the dark? She'll know."

"Listen, if you don't want to do it, take the wastebasket and garbage pan back in the house."

Beth was getting fidgety. She walked back and forth and kept saying, "I don't think we should. It's almost eight o'clock."

"Okay, good, then go back in the house."

"No, I'm going with you. I want to find out if Mim has found a way for you, me and Daddy to live together."

"We better hurry. Remember, the only reason I want to go to Mim's is for the cheerleading, remember? The move can wait until another time."

They cut through the back gate leading to Mim's yard. A dog barked, but Ruthie knew him. He was the Australian Sheep dog that belonged to the Robinsons across the street. He visited all the neighborhood yards. She said, "Spike it's me, Ruthie. Good boy," as she scratched his ears. He stopped. A few fireflies were still hanging on to the last signs of summer. They reminded Ruthie of their mother when they sat on the small porch in Huff's Neck.

They tiptoed through some bushes near Mim's back gate and finally arrived at her porch. The light was on in the kitchen.

Ruthie knocked on the back door. Mr. Nicol, Mim's husband, answered. "Well, well, if it isn't the two pups from down the street." His fat belly was sticking out of a white tee shirt, but his white hair was neatly combed. Ruthie smelled beer and something that smelled like left over frying.

Ruthie said, "We need to talk to Mim." She didn't care anymore that he called her a pup. He always did that, so she expected it.

He called, "Hey, Mim, those two pups from up the street are here to see you."

She said, "Oh, good, send them in here." She was in the living room. Ruthie was glad, because they could sit in their familiar place. She hurried in with Beth close behind.

Mr. Nicol said, "Does Emily know you're here?"

"Yes," Beth lied.

He said, "I'll bet."

They kept on walking toward down the hall to the living room where they headed straight for the small sofa.

Mim said, "Girls, I'm tired tonight. I had a hectic day so excuse me if I don't get up." She was in a light purple bathrobe sitting on a larger sofa. She had very big white fluffy slippers on her feet.

"What are you doing here at this time of the night?"

Ruthie said, "We have to hurry, because we sneaked through the back yard. I had to tell you I was picked for cheerleading today, and Emily was furious."

Beth added, "She was only a Brownie, you know. I was wondering if you found out about us living with Daddy?"

Mim smiled and said, "Girls, slow down. One thing at a time, please." She was her usual happy self.

The stray gray hair had escaped again. Ruthie took that as a good sign.

"First, Ruthie, I am so happy about the cheerleading. I promised to help you with the uniform, and that still goes. I think you should ask Emily first."

"I don't want to do that. I was wondering if you could do it, and I can pretend it came from the school."

Mim thought for a moment and said, "I guess we could do it that way. It may cause me some trouble with Emily, but I think I can handle it. Let me know how much you need. But you can count on me." She winked at Ruthie and turned to Beth.

"Now, young lady about the living arrangements. I am going to contact your father this week and then I think it would be wise if he and I have a talk with Emily."

Beth said, "You can't talk to her, she just screams. Talk to Harry instead."

"Gee, that might be the way to handle it after all. Come back Friday after school, and I will have some information by then. Will that work?"

Beth jumped up and rushed to Mim. She hugged her and said, "You are so good. I knew you'd work it out. Thank you." She kissed her cheek.

Mim squeezed her and said, "I'll try."

Ruthie stood up and said, "We better hurry out the back. We were supposed to be emptying the trash and garbage."

They each kissed her cheek and headed down the hall to the kitchen door.

Mr. Nicol was at the kitchen table drinking beer.

He said, "Well, the two pups again. I bet Emily doesn't know you're here."

Beth lied again, "Yes, she does."

They said goodbye and went towards the back yard.

Beth said, "What if he tells Emily. What if he calls her on the phone right now? I wish he would stop calling us pups."

Ruthie said, "He won't call. Mim would be too upset. I think he calls people he likes pups. It's like a nickname,"

Spike met them at the gate. They petted him and walked into their yard.

Ruthie said, "I'll handle Emily when we get in. All you have to do is be quiet."

"Alright."

Sure enough, at the top of the stairs, Emily was waiting. "Where have you been? Since when does it take nearly an entire hour to empty garbage and trash?"

Ruthie decided not to lie, she said, "We went through the back yard to Mim's house."

"Oh, that' just great. It's a little late for an unannounced visit, isn't it? I think it's a little rude, myself."

Beth said, "It wasn't rude, she was happy to see us."

"Well, the next time, you do something like this at night, you better ask me first."

Ruthie said, "Okay, you're right."

Then she decided to bring up the uniform. She thought it was a good time, because Harry was still around.

She said, bluntly, "Emily, I forgot to tell you I will need some money for the cheerleading uniform."

Beth moved to a corner of the kitchen as though to avoid a huge quarrel. She stood in the doorway of the pantry.

Emily said, "You what? That's great! Now, you spring it on me. This puts a different light on it. I may go to the school and have you removed, myself."

Beth screamed, "That's because you were just a Brownie, Emily."

Harry came into the kitchen wearing a black and white checkered robe before Emily could attack Beth. He said, "Emily, you are not doing any such thing. I told you, already, these kids have been through enough."

Emily shrunk back a little and didn't say anything.

But Harry continued as he turned to Ruthie, "Ruthie, we'll get the uniform. Don't worry about it. Let us know when you need it and what you need."

To Beth he said, "Beth, don't mention the Brownies again. That's not nice."

She said, "I won't. But she always picks on us."

"It doesn't help to say things like that back."

Ruthie said, "Thank you, Harry. I am so happy. Thank you."

They left to go upstairs to finish their homework.

Up in their bedroom, Beth flopped on the bed. "Gee, Ruthie, I thought you had that fixed with Mim? I'm glad you did it, though, because it looks like Harry is the one we can go to about moving in with Daddy.

"Now, I don't have to go to Miss Waddell or Mim for the money. Beth, I could have killed you when you brought up the Brownies. Stop doing that. Harry is our friend. I am not sure how he'll be about the move, though, but I think Mim could talk to him. She can't talk to Emily. Emily will accuse us of going to neighbors when she said not to. Now, I don't have to go to Miss Waddell or Mim for the money."

"Yeah, but you better do everything before Harry goes back to the Navy."

Chapter 30

Ruthie usually got up at seven o'clock to get ready for school, but this day was important, so she was out of bed at six thirty. She would be getting the cost of her cheerleading uniform, but more crucial was getting the details of the uniform itself. She was anxious to learn when the first day to wear it would be. She kept biting her bottom lip. Was it true that she would learn the new cheers? What if Emily was angry again about staying after school with the squad. She couldn't think about that now.

She was dressed and ready for breakfast at seven fifteen. When she walked into the kitchen, Emily said, "What are you doing up so early? Or should I ask you what you are planning to sneak behind my back today?"

"I'm not sneaking at anything. I have to get the cheerleading information today, and Miss Cash asked the squad to meet in the gym before class."

There was a soft knock at the door. Emily said, "See who that is. It's awfully early."

Ruthie opened the door and said, "Hi, Marianne, come in." In walked Marianne beaming. She was wearing a red skirt and a navy sweater that complimented her hair tied back in a pony tail.

She said, "Hi", and then, "Good Morning Emily, isn't it wonderful about us getting picked for the cheerleading?"

Emily responded, "Good Morning, Marianne. Yeah, it's really wonderful."

Ruthie felt the tension, grabbed a piece of toast. Gulped some juice and said, "Come on Marianne, we have to go. Bye, Emily. I might have practice after school, but I'll come right home after that."

Emily grudgingly said, "I should hope so. I'll get Beth to go to the store. Bye."

Ruthie and Marianne went down the back stairs silently. Once outside they jumped up and down in the driveway, because they could no longer contain their excitement. Then they started to head up the street towards school. It was a bright autumn morning with a full sun shining and a few leaves still clinging to the trees.

Marianne said, "I take it she was upset, right?"

"Yeah, she blew her top. I told her about being picked. She said I couldn't and that I could just go to the school and resign. Harry rescued me. He told her no such thing was going to happen. He even said he was happy for me."

"Wow. He's the one to have around."

"I haven't finished. Later on, I asked for the money for the uniform. She flipped out again and threatened to go to the school and resign for me. Harry stepped in again. So I am getting the money and I don't have to quit. I am so glad I don't have to lie and sneak around any more."

"Yeah, it's great. Until the next thing." "Don't hold your breath. That's just around the corner. Remember how I told you Beth and I were going to try to move in with my father? Well, Mim is putting that in the works this week. So it doesn't look like things will be quieted down for awhile."

"All I can say I hope you don't move."

They reached the First Parish Church, crossed Hancock Street and headed into the schoolyard.

Different kids came up to congratulate them.

One girl, Mary Calhoun said, "Ruthie, I see you made it. I heard the only reason was because Miss Cash felt sorry for you. Good luck anyway. Most of the kids are upset."

Marianne said, "Gee, Mary, that's not very nice. Come on, Ruthie; just ignore it. We have to get to the gym."

Ruthie felt like crying. As they walked downstairs to the gym, she said, "Gosh, I wonder why she said those things. I feel awful"

"Don't. Everyone knows she's jealous of everything and everyone. Did you see her at the tryouts? She was obnoxious. Just because she's pretty and smart, she thinks she can do and say anything.".

"I didn't see her at the tryouts. I didn't know she was like that at all."

When they got into the gym, Miss Cash handed them sheets of paper. She said, "Everyone take a place on the bleachers. I want to go over a few things with you. We don't have much time, because class starts in ten minutes. Practice will be today right after school and then every Monday and Thursday until the sports seasons are over. On the paper you will see the cost and style of the uniform. A simple maroon skirt with a yellow sweater with the letter C stitched on the front. All I need are your sizes and 25.00 to cover the costs. I'll give you more information on that, later. Please hold any questions until the practice this afternoon. You are dismissed."

Ruthie and Marianne headed to their class. Marianne said, "Don't forget lunch."

"Okay, I'll be there."

On the way to class Ruthie kept going over the things Mary Calhoun had said. She tried not to be upset. What if she hadn't been picked; she'd be upset, too. But she didn't think she'd be mean about it.

She opened the door to Miss Waddell's English class. As she stepped inside, all the kids were standing and clapping. Ruthie heard "Nice going, Ruthie." "The school has a new mascot."

Ruthie forgot all about Mary Calhoun.

Chapter 31

At the first practice, Miss Cash said, "Girls, please be prompt for practice next Monday when the uniforms will be distributed. You will wear them to school the following Wednesday for the first football game at Milton High."

Ruthie poked Marianne and said, "I can't wait."

"Me, too, won't it be fun?"

Other comments Ruthie overheard were, "Wow, that's great, and where do we get on the bus?"

Miss Cash, "You will catch the bus outside the gym door promptly at 2:30."

Ruthie whispered to Marianne, "Emily will flip out over the games."

"You better tell her while Harry is still home. How long does he have?"

"Around a little over a week."

Miss Cash assembled the girls. "Girls break into small groups and learn the cheers you will be using at the first game. The personal cheers are very easy, but there are some others that are longer."

Girls shuffled around the gym and wound up into groups of six. The leader in Ruthie's group asked, "Ruthie, do you mind getting on top of the pyramids? You are the designated mascot."

"No, I figured I would be doing that. It sounds like fun."

"Okay, we won't be doing those until we have a full practice, probably next week. So the first cheer to learn is: We've got the coach, we've got the team, we've got the pep, we've got the steam, coach, team, pep, steam, we're on the beam."

They recited it together and Ruthie was so excited at how well they sounded. Miss Cash blew a whistle, "Squad dismissed until the practice on Thursday after school."

Ruthie looked at the clock. Four thirty. Emily would be enraged. She hurried over to Marianne, "Get your things. I have to get out of here. Emily will be so upset if I am late setting the table."

"We can take the bus. I have a bus ticket. You can use it."

"Gee, thanks. I'll pay you back as soon as I get my allowance."

"Don't worry about it. Let's go."

On the way to the bus stop, they practiced the cheer they had heard. The bus was on time. Ruthie was relieved because they could get home by five fifteen in time to set the table. She dreaded any confrontation with Emily. She decided to talk to Harry about the practices and the games so it could be settled before he left for his ship.

They had two blocks to walk after the bus stopped at their street. Ruthie hurried ahead and called over her shoulder, "Thanks, Marianne, see you in the morning."

"Okay. Bye."

When Ruthie entered the kitchen, Emily was at the stove. Ruthie smelled meatloaf. Yuck.

Emily said, "Well, here's the star of the school."

Harry was sitting at the kitchen table. "Hey, Emily, stop it before it even gets started."

Ruthie said nothing. She washed her hands and proceeded to set the table.

Halfway through supper the phone rang, Beth rushed to answer it and said, "Ruthie, it's for you. Some guy named, Frank."

Ruthie excused her self from the table, she said, "I'll find out." She took the receiver but couldn't imagine why it would be Frank calling. He was too popular. GOOD. Beth made a istake. She said, "Hello."

"Hi Ruthie. I'm having a party Friday night and I was wondering if you'd like to come?"

She was giddy with excitement. Frank was so popular. He was also very good looking with dark hair and light blue eyes. Emily would have something else to rave about if she found out he is Italian

"It sounds great, but I'll have to ask. Just a minute."

She came to the dining room. Emily said, "This is rude. Now what is it?"

"Frank wants to know if I can go to his party Friday night."

"No. Tell him no."

Harry said, "Ruthie you can go. Emily, why are you doing this?"

Ruthie went back to the phone, "Hi Frank, yes, I can go. Thank you."

"Great, see you there, seven o'clock."

She dreaded going back into the dining room. Harry was in control. Ruthie heard him say, "Emily you and I are having a talk later. We have to settle things with these girls before I leave." Emily was meek, "Okay. But these kids shouldn't call during supper."

Beth said, "They don't know when we eat."

Harry said, "Beth, don't use that tone. I said we'll settle things later."

When supper was over, Beth and Ruthie cleared things up while Emily and Harry went to the living room. She and Beth tried to eavesdrop. They couldn't hear everything, only some sentences. Emily said, "Ruthie drives me crazy, she thinks she's so popular at school." Then Harry said, "Emily, for God's sake, give her a break. She's only a kid and she is trying to have some fun. Look at what both of them have been through."

Emily said, "Is that going to be thrown up forever———" Then she and Harry began to whisper.

When the kitchen was cleared, Beth and Ruthie headed upstairs to finish homework. On the way, Ruthie said, "I'll show you the new cheer we learned today. I can't wait to go to that party Friday night. Can I wear your pink sweater?"

"Okay, as long as you don't showoff too much. I hope you save some time so we can find out from Mim about living with Daddy. Yes, you can wear the sweater."

"We can go to Mim's tomorrow. I can meet you in front of the tree at three o'clock."

"I can't wait. Do you think she was able to do it?"

"I don't know. I'm not counting on it. I keep wondering if Emily will go back to her old ways once Harry goes back to his ship."

Chapter 32

Ruthie turned over in bed the next morning, stretched and thought of the things that were going to happen that day. How was she going to tell Marianne about the invite to Frank's party. What if Marianne wasn't invited? She'd be hurt. Ruthie was not sure if Marianne was attracted to Frank. Her raving about his clothes, what a good dancer he was and his athletics at first base seemed suspicious. GOOD I LIKE THIS Ruthie looked at the clock, 6:45, and jumped out of bed. She twisted her lip and rifled through the closet for her red corduroy suit. She might run into Frank in the hall. Oh, and she had to remember to tell Marianne she couldn't walk home after school, because of the meeting at Mim's. What if Mim found out she and Beth could live with their father, they'd have to move.

She hurried downstairs to the kitchen and the awful oatmeal; Emily was drinking coffee at the table. "Hi Ruthie. You're up early again. I guess you have a lot going on in school, huh? Don't worry about being late getting home this afternoon." Ruthie thought something has changed; she's really being nice.

Her insides rumbled so much, she was afraid Emily could actually hear them. Her nerves again. GOOD What was going on? Was it the talk Harry had the night before with Emily? Whatever happened, it worked, wow, for how long? It was nice to start the day like that, maybe the rest of the day would go good, too.

"Yes, I do, but I'll get through as soon as I can." She felt a little guilty, because she would be sneaking to see Mim. But what if the move didn't work out? It might be okay if Emily continued to be pleasant. GOOD

"I guess you must be excited to be invited to the party Friday night. I met Frank's mother once, and she seemed very nice. Emily dropped her neck into her hands and changed her voice. Harry is leaving next Wednesday, and I am really going to miss him."

She sounded teary.

Ruthie said, "Beth and I will, too. We'll help you every way we can. I have to get going, Marianne will be waiting. I'll be home as soon as I finish everything."

"Okay, have fun."

Ruthie felt insecure with all the friendliness Emily had shown. She was confused by this new happiness and worried about how long it would last. Emily could turn her niceness on and off. GOODShe was always friendly around Mim. As Ruthie headed down the stairs to meet Marianne, she thought about the party invitation.

Marianne was waiting at the end of the driveway, she yelled, "Hi Ruthie, I have some great news."

"Hi."

Mariannne said, "Isn't it great about being invited to Frank's Friday night. He said he had called you, and that you were going. What are you wearing?"

Ruthie was overjoyed. She grabbed Marianne and gave her a hug. Whew, one less thing to worry about. Great. "Yeah, I was shocked, were you? I'm borrowing Beth's pink sweater. I hope she doesn't mess it up between now and then. What are you wearing?"

"I'm borrowing my brother's white sweater. He doesn't like me to wear his sweaters, because he said I make bumps in the front, but I begged him and he finally gave in."

They hurried along Hancock Street. Ruthie said, "Emily is so different, actually sociable to me this morning. Harry had a talk with her; it must have worked. She even said not to worry about getting home late after school. And, if that weren't enough, she said she had met Frank's mother. She liked her."

"Hey, listen, Frank said Mary Calhoun is going, too. How is that going to work?"

"I'm steering clear of her after what she said about the cheerleading. I'm meeting Beth to go to Mim's after school. I felt a little guilty after Emily was so nice, but I have to get things settled, Harry is leaving next Wednesday."

"Ruthie, don't mess anything up. Play it cool."

They arrived at school; Mary Calhoun was waiting near the door. Marianne said, "Speak of the devil."

She was prettier than Ruthie realized. Her blonde hair was carefully combed as usual. It was so perfect, Ruthie wondered if her mother combed it everyday. Her mother did own a beauty shop. Mary had the best clothes in the school. She had clothes for everything. Gosh, she even wore angora socks.

Mary rushed toward Marianne and Ruthie and said, "I hear you two have been invited to Frank's party. I guess it's because you live so close and all, you know inviting kids in the neighborhood."

Marianne poked Ruthie and said, "Yeah, we figured it was because of that or maybe his mother made him invite us."

Ruthie bit her cheek hard to keep from being convulsed. His mother didn't even know them. Saved by the bell, which rang for homeroom class.

As Ruthie hurried down the hall, she ran into Frank, who said, "Hey, where are you rushing to, firecracker?" He looked gorgeous even though his dark hair had a wind blown look. He wore a maroon shirt and gray pants. He had beautiful white teeth.

Ruthie felt her face redden. Firecracker, she loved it. "Thanks for the invitation. It sounds like a lot of fun."

"Well, it's going to more fun with you there. I'm glad you can come."

"So am I. I'm late. I have to run, see you Friday." She headed for her classroom.

After she was settled at her desk, she started thinking about Mary Calhoun. She couldn't figure out why Mary was so insulting. Could Mary know she was attracted to Frank? Ruthie felt her face flush again, and she failed to hear Miss Cash call her name in roll call.

It wasn't until Miss Cash said, "I guess Ruthie Brooks is somewhere else," and the burst of laughter from the class that Ruthie realized she has been far away.

At 2:30 Ruthie rushed to Marianne and said, "I have to hurry, because I'm meeting Beth at the tree, and I don't know how long we'll be at Mim's. So, I'll see you tomorrow morning."

"Okay. Stay cool."

"I will." Ruthie hurried away.

She managed to get to the tree at three o'clock. Beth was waiting and was upset again that Ruthie might not come. She settled down and they walked up the steps and knocked on the door. Mim, still in her nurse's uniform answered, scooped them in her arms and said, "I'm so glad you're here. Come on in. I have some cookies and milk set out for you."

Impulsive Beth wrung her hands and let it slip, "What did you find out? Can we go and live with Daddy and Mrs. Alexander?"

"Come in and sit down so I can explain things."

Beth insisted, "Can we?"

"No, it didn't work out."

Beth began to cry and said, "I can't stay with Emily, she's mean."

"I spoke to your father and Mrs. Alexander, both. We decided it would do more harm to your relationship with Emily, and your father's relationship with her. He is hoping to be able to talk with her without a confrontation. We decided that could never happen if he asked you to come and live with him."

Ruthie put her arm around Beth's shoulder, and explained, "It's not Mim's fault. Emily was a friend this morning, and we should give her a chance. We have each other, and I think it could work since Harry had the talk with her."

"No, it won't. Remember she was only a Brownie and she takes it out on us."

The girls were now in the living room on the familiar sofa. They left the cookies and milk untouched.

Mim said, "Your father was going to try to speak to Emily one more time, but since Harry has done that, he won't have to. It could get her upset again, so I'll make sure he doesn't approach Emily. Eat your cookies, and drink your milk. I'll be here for you anytime you need me."

Ruthie said, "Thank you, Mim for what you tried to do." She poked Beth who reluctantly echoed her sentiments.

She said, "So, we'll still be pups? And we can come here anytime we want? Will you be friends with Emily so we wont' have to sneak?'

"Okay, I'll work on that right away."

Beth jumped up and hugged Mim, hard. She pushed the familiar stray hair out of her eyes.

Mim laughed. "It's my trade mark, everyone notices it. What other news do you have, any?"

Beth spoke first, "Yup, Ruthie is going to a party Friday night, thanks to Harry. We forgot to tell you, he's leaving next Wednesday."

Ruthie said, "Marianne and I have been invited. We are really excited, because Frank is one of the popular kids. There's a girl, Mary Calhoun who has been sort of mean and she has been invited. She's beautiful and has tons of pretty clothes. She said probably the only reason we were invited is because we live in the neighborhood."

"It sounds like jealously. Jealousy is not good. If you ever think you're doing something out of jealousy, stop, and get your self in control. It can be one of the worst habits to form. Now, it's getting near four thirty, you better be going. You don't want to take advantage of Emily's new attitude. I'll try to fix it so you won't have to sneak."

Beth jumped up and said, "Oooh, we better go."

Mim walked to the door with them. "Bye, come back anytime. Ruthie be friendly with that girl, but don't get too involved."

"I try to be friendly, but she hurts my feelings."

"I know, just be careful."

Chapter 33

Friday finally came. In the morning, Ruthie's hair was a limp mess. The sweater she wanted to borrow from Beth had gum stuck on the front. Ruthie was furious with Beth. How could she be so stupid as to get gum on the sweater? She hoped she never got it out. What could she wear in its place? She was so jumpy, in desperation; she decided to ask Emily for help. She went downstairs and told Emily her dilemma. Emily was sitting in a chair, knitting beside the window in the kitchen. She was dressed in a tweed skirt and sweater as if she were going out. That intimidated Ruthie. She was afraid Emily would be perturbed. But she finally said, "Emily something awful happened. Beth got gum on the sweater I was going to wear to the party tonight."

Emily said, "Don't worry about it. I'm going shopping today and I'll see if I can get another one like it." Emily was accommodating, Ruthie thought. "Wow, this is a change."

"Gee, you will? What if you can't find one?"

"I'll get a white one. You can wear it with your navy skirt. It'll look great."

"Wow, thank you, Emily. I'll go finish getting ready for school."

She thought Harry must have been really hard on her when he gave her the talk and that it wouldn't last. She was only a Brownie, and that got her. Navy with a white sweater, gee that's better than the pink one anyway. She finished getting ready for school and blushed thinking about Frank. What if he asked her to dance?

Back in the kitchen, she grabbed a piece of toast and a glass of juice.

She called to Emily, "I'm leaving now to meet Marianne. Thank you for the help. It's great. Bye."

Emily called from the other room, "Don't worry about anything, you'll look fine. I'll go shopping this morning. I'll see you this afternoon, bye."

Ruthie was so excited to tell Marianne how great Emily was acting. She hurried to where Marianne was waiting in her usual spot.

"Hey, Marianne, guess what? Beth got gum on the pink sweater. When I told Emily she offered to go shopping to get one like it. She even said if she couldn't find one, she'd get a white one to wear with my navy skirt. She's acting so nice; it makes everything so much easier. It won't last. She has a mean streak. I'm going to enjoy it while it lasts."

"Wow, that is a switch. Don't get her upset. I feel like I'm getting a sore throat. She cleared her throat and coughed a little. I can't wait for tonight"

"Me too, we can just walk to Frank's house. Your throat might be sore if you slept with your mouth open."

"Yeah, that's what I thought, too. I hope you're right. She cleared her throat, again and sniffed."

They passed the ball field.

Marianne said, "We better step on it, we're later than usual"

When they reached the schoolyard, Mary Calhoun was talking to Frank.

Ruthie's heart beat faster. It was true; Mary Calhoun was crazy about him. She was really flirting with him. But, when Ruthie waved, he came towards them and left Mary standing alone.

"Hi, Ruthie, Hi Marianne, all set for tonight? My mother made some great stuff to eat; you know chocolate chip cookies, fudge, chips all that stuff. My dad set up the music. They rolled up the rug in the dining room so we can dance. He even stacked a bunch of recordings and dimmed the lights. It should be fun."

Ruthie said, "Gosh your parents are doing a lot, aren't they?" She wondered if she and Beth were living with their mother and father if they would have parties.

"Yeah, they like me to bring my friends to our house. Well, I have to run before the bell."

Marianne and Ruthie headed for their class, too.

The rest of the day dragged. Finally it was 2:30. On the way home, Ruthie told Marianne, "Let's hurry so I can see my new sweater. Come to my house so you can see it, too."

"Okay. I am really beginning to feel crappy." She continued to cough a little and clear her throat.

"Aw, it's nothing."

When they arrived at Ruthie's house, they rushed into the kitchen. There hanging on a hanger was the sweater of sweaters, soft white and beautiful.

Marianne said, "Wow, Ruthie, you are so lucky. It feels so cuddily."

Ruthie held the sweater up to check the fit and said, "Look at the label, it has angora in it, I love it."

Emily was standing in the doorway. She said, "I was fortunate to get it, because it was the last one in your size. I'm glad you like it. Was I right, won't it look good with your navy skirt?"

"Yes, it's perfect. Thank you." What was going on with her?

Marianne said, "You did a great job, Emily. It's nice. Well, I have to go, my mother will be looking for me. I'll see you tonight. I'll come by around fifteen till seven."

"Okay, I can't wait. See you then. Three hours and 15 minutes."

At fifteen till seven, Marianne hadn't shown up. Ruthie called her house and found out she was sick in bed. Oh, no now she'd have to go alone. She dreaded walking into the party alone—everyone else would have come with someone.

Harry came in to the hall near the telephone. He said, "Is there a problem? I thought you had a party to go to."

"Yeah, I do, but Marianne is sick so I have to alone."

"So? Just go in alone. It's not a big deal. Nobody will notice you came alone."

"Okay, I'll do it. Thanks, Harry."

"Get going. Have a good time."

Marianne headed out the door. She began thinking about Mary Calhoun and the remarks she'd probably make. She began thinking about Frank. He was always friendly. Maybe Harry was right. Going alone wasn't. a big deal. She went up the steps to Frank's front porch. He lived in a brick house, like the others in the neighborhood. The only difference was his mother had a beautiful rose garden that everyone admired.

Frank answered the door and took her into the dining room where other kids were dancing. Ruthie looked around and saw Mary Calhoun with Chuck Moody. Frank took her coat and said, "Wait till I put this with the other coats, and we can dance."

Ruthie was glad the lights were sort of dim, because her face was very red, she could feel it.

Mary Calhoun walked up and said, "Wow, where's your best friend? I thought you two were inseparable. I noticed you came alone. I thought you were the Bobsey Twins. I came with Chuck. You can have Frank."

"Marianne is sick with a sore throat. She couldn't come."

"Aww. Isn't that a shame?"

Frank stepped up, took Ruthie's hand and led her to the dance area. Ruthie said, "I feel so uncomfortable around Mary. I don't think she likes me."

He said, "Oh, she's probably jealous. She treats anyone who she thinks is better dressed, smarter, whatever mean. Don't let her know it bothers you or it'll get worse. I know her pretty well."

"Gee, I don't feel so bad. I didn't realize it."

"Oh, yeah. I'm surprised you didn't know it. I don't know how a nice guy like Chuck can stand her."

"Does she go with Chuck?"

"Pretty much. Their families belong to the same yacht club."

Ruthie and Frank danced together most of the evening, except when Chuck asked her for one dance when Frank went to get more Cokes. Mary came up to them and said, "I'm back Chuck." She sounded angry.

Chuck said, "Thanks Ruthie, maybe after a few more songs, we'll dance again."

Mary took his hand and said, "Come on, Chuck. *We* came together, remember?" They moved across the dance floor.

Eleven o'clock came too fast for Ruthie. It was a perfect night, only maybe she shouldn't have had that one dance with Chuck. What if Mary caused trouble for me like spreading gossip that wasn 't true?

She said, as everyone gathered at the front door, "This has been great, Frank, thank you again."

"You bet, be good firecracker."

Ruthie's heart jumped. Just as she headed out the door, Mary Calhoun stepped out of a corner in the hall. She said, "Hey, Ruthie, wait, I have something important to tell you."

"Okay. What is it?" She thought here it comes. Trouble.

"Chuck told me you couldn't be trusted as a friend. I thought you should know that. I think he knows you're a flirt."

Ruthie's eyes filled, but the light was dim, so it went unnoticed. She said, "Did he say why?"

"No, just not to trust you."

"What did I do?"

"I don't know? Too much flirting, maybe."

When Ruthie reached the sidewalk, no one was around. She cried hard as she hurried home. Nobody likes me. What'll I do? I wish Marianne were here so she could have helped me with this mess.

When she arrived in the kitchen, Harry was there. "Hey, what's the matter? Didn't you have a good time?

Ruthie sniffed as she explained. "Yes, I did but Mary Calhoun told me her boyfriend, Chuck said not to trust me as a friend. It was awful. She didn't even tell me why. All she said was I was a flirt." Ruthie wept.

"Hey, look. Don't be so upset. Ask Chuck to explain it. Forget that girl. Go directly to the source. As long as you know you didn't do anything to deserve the comment, try to forget it until you can talk to him. Now go to bed, and try to get some rest."

"Thank you, Harry. Night."

"Night, Ruthie."

Ruthie cried off and on while she was getting ready for bed. Harry was nice; it made her cry a little more. Then she heard a clear voice, "Always have a plan." It was her mother.

She decided to talk to Chuck like Harry said. But when did she ever see him alone? At track and field he always had other kids around. She'd get him aside at Christian Endeavor next Sunday night. She wasn't sure she could wait until then.

She whispered, "Thank you, Mama. I love you."

She nestled under the covers and thought about how nice it was to have Harry around. He was leaving Wednesday.

Chapter 34

On Saturday morning, Ruthie was up and dressed by eight-thirty. She went down to the kitchen where the smell of coffee and pancakes were in the air. She was hungry, but felt nervous, not wanting to eat due to the remarks made by Mary Calhoun the night before at Frank's party.

Emily said, "Gee, you're up early."

"Yeah, I know I am, but I couldn't sleep. The remarks about me not being trusted as a friend kept going over and over in my head and kept me wake."

"Well, once you confront Chuck, maybe you can get it settled. Accusations like that are always hurtful. Did you tell Marianne, yet? I was hoping she might know something about why he supposedly said it."

"No, she's still sick. I decided to go to Christian Endeavor Sunday to ask Chuck. I'm scared. He's nice, but I want to be careful not to say anything that will make him think I'm accusing him."

"Sit down, and have some pancakes. Get yourself some juice, and we can talk about how to approach him."

"Okay, but I don't feel like eating anything. I'll try." Ruthie headed to the refrigerator, poured herself some juice and sat down at the kitchen table.

Emily poured herself another cup of coffee and sat opposite Ruthie.

She said, "Just call him to a spot where nobody can hear you. That might make it easier. Get to the point right away, if you can. What you were planning?"

"I was going to say, "Hey, Chuck, can I ask you something?"

"That sounds good."

"Then, Mary Calhoun told me you said I couldn't be trusted as a friend. I was wondering what I did." Ruthie played with her pancakes.

Beth, still in her pajamas came into the kitchen. "What are you talking about? Or is it a big secret?"

Emily said, "I'm trying to help Ruthie get to the bottom of the remark that Mary Calhoun made."

"Oh, that's no secret, probably everyone knows that thing. Ruthie never stops talking about it since it happened."

Then to Ruthie, "Forget about it. Who cares about Mary Calhoun and this Chuck whoever he is. They're both stuck up."

"Mind your own business. Who asked you anyway?" Ruthie began to cry.

Emily said, "Beth, be a little nicer to your sister. Please, her feelings are hurt."

"Well, why didn't she get it solved before she left the party? Why didn't she get Chuck to make Mary Calhoun explain it? Then it would be over. I'm sick of listening about it."

Ruthie sprung out of her chair, "Yeah, well then don't. If anyone ever does something to you, I don't want to hear about it. Of course if that happens, that will be a huge tragedy."

Beth said, "No, it won't. Kids do rotten stuff to me all the time."

Emily stepped in. "Alright, that's enough. Beth sit down, and eat your breakfast and then get dressed."

"Okay, but are we going to have to hear about this forever? I'll call Mary Calhoun and get it fixed right now."

Ruthie shouted, "No, you will not. Emily, tell her to stop."

Emily, ignored Beth and continued, "Ruthie, don't practice what to say to Chuck too much or it'll sound stiff. Does that make sense?"

"Yes. I'll just call him aside like we said."

Beth continued, "That's what you get going to Frank's party. You thought you were so big."

Emily shot Beth a look and said, "That's enough."

When everyone was finished with breakfast, Ruthie and Beth cleared the table and prepared to wash the dishes.

Beth said, "Emily, Ruthie didn't finish."

"Leave her alone or I'll have to punish you."

What if Emily started acting like she did before she had the talks with Harry?

Chapter 35

Ruthie had a miserable weekend, except that when she called Marianne and learned she was well enough to come over to talk. Around 1 o'clock on Sunday afternoon, Marianne knocked on the kitchen door. Ruthie sprang to answer.

Marianne wearing a heavy coat came in and said, "Wow, how was the party? Did you have a good time? Did you dance with Frank?"

"Yes, it was great and we danced almost every dance, except for one, and I danced that with Chuck Moody."

"Oh, oh, you mean the Chuck who has been dating Mary Calhoun?"

"Yeah, and at the end of the party Mary told me he said I couldn't be trusted so I wouldn't be a good friend."

"Jealous, pure and simple."

"I cried all the way home. Do have any idea why he would say that?"

"You mean *if* he said it, don't you?"

"Gee, she wouldn't just make that up would she?"

"I don't know her very well, personally, but I've heard she says terrible things behind people's backs. Remember when she said Cynthia Campbell's mother was a drunk? So, are you going to let her get away with it?"

Beth, who obviously had been eavesdropping, came into the kitchen. She said, "Marianne, Ruthie could have settled this at the party. She should have called Chuck and Mary together and asked him right then. But, no we've had to listen to her moan and groan about her hurt feelings."

"Beth, mind your business or I'll call Emily. Now, get out of here."

Ruthie turned to Marianne and said, "Let's go up to my room so we don't have to listen to her."

"It's not *your* room, it's mine, too."

"Come on, Marianne." They left Beth alone in the kitchen.

Once they were settled in the bedroom, Marianne said, "What are you going to do, anything?"

"I didn't know Mary had called Cynthia's mother a drunk. I know her, she's far from it. I'm going to Christian Endeavor Sunday night to talk to Chuck and find out for myself."

"Alone? I don't think I can go with you. My parents think I should stick around the house because of this cold."

"Yeah, I'm going alone. I'm just going to get Chuck aside and ask him straight out. I'm a little scared because I don't know him very well. Frank says he's a nice guy. If that's right, I think I can talk to him."

Marianne looked at the clock. "I have to go. I said I'd be gone only a little while. If I can go to CE, do you want me to go with you?" Marianne headed down the hall to the stairs.

"It's okay, I think I can do it alone. I'll let you know what happens."

Ruthie walked down the hall behind Marianne towards the kitchen door. When they walked through the kitchen, Beth, still there, said, "Did you two get the world's biggest problem settled?"

Ruthie said, "Marianne, ignore her. I'll let you know what happens. Thanks for coming over. Bye."

"Okay. Bye."

When Marianne had gone, Ruthie said, "You know what? I hope you never get your feelings hurt." She left the kitchen.

Back in her room, she rifled through her closet looking for a nice outfit to wear when she spoke to Chuck. If Mary were there, she wanted to look the best she could. Mary would probably have a new terrific outfit to wear, with her angora socks, of course. She chose a navy sweater and red skirt.

She flopped on the bed and decided to take a nap until suppertime.

Ruthie dressed carefully and left her house at 6:30. Maybe she could corner Chuck. When she arrived at the church, it was too close to seven o'clock so she would have to wait until the meeting ended. She was nervous through the meeting and kept chewing her lip and picking at her cuticles. She watched the back of Mary Calhoun in a new green plaid dress. Joan Crosby was there and a few other people Ruthie knew. Frank wasn't there. There were only two speakers tonight, sometimes there were three or four. The topics were about the same how to become a more dedicated Christian.

Once the last speaker finished, Ruthie rushed to the hall and waited for Chuck. The church was dimly lit, and it appeared even darker because of the gray walls and dark woodwork. Chuck was one of the last ones to come out. Mary Calhoun was right behind him. He wore his white track sweater with the big blue Q on the front.

Ruthie stepped near him and said, "Hi Chuck. Can you come over here I want to ask you something?" Mary watched, but said nothing.

"Sure, what's up?" Ruthie felt comfortable, because he smiled down at her and leaned against his arm on the wall.

"The other night at Frank's party, Mary Calhoun told me you said I couldn't be trusted and wouldn't make a good friend. What have I done?"

Ruthie could tell by the look on his face, it didn't happen. She was elated even before he answered.

"She said *what*? Pathetic. I didn't say anything about you to her or anyone." He shook his head in disgust.

Ruthie said, "Gee, I hoped you'd say that. I wanted to check with you, because my feelings were hurt."

"Well, they don't have to be, because it never happened."

"Okay, thanks, Chuck. I'll see you at school, bye."

"Sure. Bye."

Ruthie was so excited with the news; she wanted to jump and yell, "Chuck didn't say it."

A friend, Pat Boyd, came towards her. "What hit you?" Pat was pretty with long blonde hair that always looked great even on damp days when everyone else's was a mess. Tonight was no different.

Ruthie told her about Mary Calhoun and what Chuck had said.

Pat laughed and said, "Mary is so jealous of you, she can't stand it. I'm surprised you don't know that. Everyone else does."

Ruthie said, "Really? What a relief. I have to get home to tell my family."

On the way home, Ruthie tried to think about what Harry would say now. He would have said, "Be friendly, but be careful of that girl."

That was Ruthie's plan. She thought about having her mother and how much easier her life would have been. Mother's always knew what to say to make things better.

Ruthie

Chapter 36

Ruthie woke up off and on during the night. She wondered if Chuck would tell Mary about the confrontation. Would that make things worse with her? She tossed around, fell back asleep. Then woke again with a decision not to change how she acted towards Mary Calhoun. She decided to take a chance that Chuck wouldn't say anything to anyone. Hadn't he acted like he was annoyed with Mary? He didn't seem like the type to drag things on. She was happy with the situation now and wasn't that all she wanted to begin with?

Her alarm went off at seven o'clock. She jumped out of bed so she'd have time to dress carefully. Today was cheerleading day so she'd wear her maroon skirt and gold sweater with the big C on it. It always made

Mary Calhoun catty when she saw Ruthie in the school outfit. Ruthie couldn't figure out why because Mary usually had on new clothes. Ruthie tried to remember if she had ever seen Mary in the same out fit even twice. No.

When she entered the kitchen, Emily was at the breakfast table drinking coffee. She said, "Hi Ruthie, I hope that girl doesn't cause any more problems."

"Me, too. I'm just going to treat her the same as I always have. I'm happy with the way it turned out when I asked Chuck, and that is all that matters to me anyway."

"Yeah, that's a good decision. Isn't she the one who was furious because you were picked for cheerleading?"

"She's the one. She's the best dressed in the school."

"It seems like people like her are never satisfied. They want everything. Anyway, things worked out good for you."

"I better get going. Marianne will be waiting for me. Have a good day."

"You, too. Mama would be proud of you, Ruthie."

On the way out the door, Ruthie couldn't help her thoughts. Even though Emily was being nice, Ruthie thought, her mother wouldn't be proud of her leaving her to die in Medfield. She hurried down the stairs as she tried to hide that thought.

It was misty out meaning limp hair for the game today. Marianne was waiting at the end of the driveway dressed in her cheerleading outfit. She had a white scarf over her head.

Ruthie said, "I didn't know it was misty like this. It feels like a fine rain. That will make my hair a mess for the game and cheerleading today."

"That's why I wore this. I didn't want mine a mess. Maybe you can fix yours. You never look bad"

"Thanks, but damp weather usually makes a mess. I'll deal with it, somehow."

When they arrived at the schoolyard, Mary Calhoun was talking with Chuck. Marianne said, "Oh, oh I hope he didn't tell her about your encounter."

"I don't think he would. He acted more like he was upset with her. Here, she comes."

Mary walked up to Marianne and Ruthie. Her face was red like she had cried, but she managed to gain composure when she said to Ruthie, "I guess you'll be happy. Chuck broke up with me. He said we're seeing too much of each other."

"Why would that make me happy? It doesn't."

"Well all I know he just told me we are seeing too much of each other."

Ruthie said, "I'm sorry. It doesn't make me happy."

"I bet."

"Marianne and I have to go so we won't miss the first bell." They headed towards the building.

On the way, Marianne said, "Wow, it couldn't have happened to a sweeter person."

"I guess he didn't say anything or she would have been angry. What a relief. I'm just going on like nothing was ever said by her."

"I'm glad you can do it. I couldn't." The hall was crowded as they made their way through the noise.

Ruthie said, "I'll see you for the game."

"Yup, bye."

Ruthie headed towards her homeroom, but couldn't help being happy that Chuck didn't mention her talk with him. She wondered if that were the real reason he broke up with Mary.

She heard a voice, "Hey firecracker, you better hurry,"

"Hi Frank, yeah it's almost time for the second bell."

In the cafeteria Ruthie, Marianne and some other girls usually got the table over in the furthest corner. At lunchtime it was the same group there. Mary Calhoun came over. Marianne said, "Ruthie, look who's coming."

Mary approached Ruthie. "So, miss cheerleader when are you going out with Chuck?"

The others in the group backed up a little, almost like a gunfight in an old western. They were silent.

"He didn't ask me.

A few snickers were heard. The silence again.

Mary said, "You know you make a horrible friend, not that I considered you a friend to begin with, but I never expected that you'd go to the trouble of breaking me and Chuck up. I might as well tell you he'd never go with you so don't bother and you won't get your feelings hurt." She walked away.

Donna, one of the regulars at lunch, spoke up, "Ruthie, are you going to let her get by with that? She's desperate."

"Well, I decided to drop it. It looks like she's made up her mind about the breakup. She doesn't like me, and I can't change that."

Marianne said, "Ruthie, sometimes you are too nice for your own good."

Something Ruthie's mother had said popped into her mind; take the low road whenever you can. The bell rang to return to class. Ruthie rushed away to hide her tears.

She thought about her father and Mim. She decided to visit them later.

Chapter 37

The next day after school, Ruthie went to Emily who was sitting by the dining room window, knitting. Emily was a beautiful seamstress and knitter. She was always calm when she was there in her favorite spot.

Ruthie said, "Emily, if you don't need anything at the store, may I go visit Mim for a little while. I haven't seen her for a long time, and I am afraid she is wondering what happened to me."

"That's okay. I don't need anything at the store today. Don't wear out your welcome."

"I won't."

Ruthie walked through the kitchen and down the back stairs. She deliberately didn't invite Beth, because of her hostile attitude about the

Mary Calhoun mess. She approached the back gate leading to Mim's back porch. She knocked on the door, Mim's husband answered.

He was wearing his familiar tee shirt, which barely covered his beer belly.

He said, "Well, the pup. I suppose you want Mim."

"Yes, if it's okay."

He called out, "Hey, Mim, one of the pups is here."

Mim hurried out and said, "Hi Ruthie. I missed you, where have you been? Isn't Beth with you? Come in."

Mim, dressed in familiar navy blue wore a white apron. She grabbed Ruthie and gave her a hug.

Ruthie said, "I have been meaning to come and see you, but a lot of stuff has happened."

They walked to the living room where the familiar small couch was waiting. Ruthie walked to it and sat down.

Mim said, "So, tell me all your news."

Ruthie said, "Do you remember when you told me to be careful of Mary Calhoun? Well, I wasn't careful enough. She told me Chuck, her boyfriend, had said I wasn't to be trusted as a friend. I cried and cried and Harry told me to ask Chuck about it. I did. He never said it.

Then he and Mary broke up. Mary confronted me in the cafeteria at lunch in front of all the other kids blaming me for the breakup. It was awful, but most of the kids took my side. Now, I just stay away from her as much as possible."

"Oh, dear these things are the lessons we all have to learn in life. Some of the time they are hurtful. I am so sorry. So Harry helped. How did Emily act?"

"She was pretty nice, too. She gave me permission to come here today, so I didn't have to sneak. Oh, and by the way, Beth has been acting awful about it, so that's why she isn't here."

"Well try not to have trouble with her over this, Ruthie. You two are good together."

Ruthie said, "You're right. She said some mean things, but now that I am talking to you, I think she was trying to help me in her own way. She said things like 'it's not a big deal, you're a baby.'"

Mim laughed a little and said, "She's young and she loves you. I saw Tom the other day and he asked me if I had seen you. I told him you were busy with school things."

"Beth and I are going to see him this week. I really miss Harry. Emily said he'll be getting out of the Navy soon and will be home for good. She has been acting pretty nice. She even bought me a new sweater for a party. I miss my mother. All the kids have mothers they can talk to. I'm glad I have you, Mim."

"That works both ways, Ruthie. I love having talks with you."

Mim's husband, Nick, called from the kitchen, "Mim, is that pup still here? I think she needs to go home."

"She's leaving in a little while."

He said, "You're wrong, Mim."

Ruthie felt sorry for Mim, she was always wrong, even about stupid stuff like dog food.

Mim told Ruthie, "That girl Mary sounds like she is unhappy and takes it out on you. Don't be angry with her, Ruthie, just try to avoid trouble with her. At your age, you encounter many painful things. It's part of growing up, unfortunately. But we all have gone through it. Crying isn't a sin. It helps relieve the sorrow."

Ruthie walked toward, Mim, took her hand, leaned over and kissed her cheek. She said, "Thank you, Mim. You are always nice. Now, I better go. Nick will be happy."

They both laughed as they walked through the kitchen. Nick was sitting at the kitchen table drinking Pickwick Ale. He glanced up and said, "Bye, you pup. Don't forget to close the gate so the dog can't get out. Mim would have to hunt her down."

"Okay, bye. Bye, Mim, see you soon."

"Bye, Mim, see you soon," mimicked Nick.

On the way to her house, Ruthie thought about Mim and Nick. She felt sorry and wondered if they loved each other.

It was nearing suppertime, so she hurried. She wanted to see her father, soon, but she would have to sneak. Emily would never give her permission to go there.

Chapter 38

As Ruthie crossed Mim's yard, she began to plan a way to see her father the next day after school. She wondered what advice he would give about Mary Calhoun. She would definitely have to sneak, because Emily never gave permission.

Beth went a lot and sneaked every time, but never was caught. Ruthie knew the reason Beth went so many times was to get money.

Ruthie came to her own back door, and decided to figure out her plan later.

When she entered the kitchen, she smelled American Chop Suey cooking. It was one meal Emily served that was good. She added green peppers and onions to canned tomatoes, and served it over elbow noodles. Everyone liked the combination.

Ruthie said, "Wow, that smells good."

Emily said, "You always like this. How was Mim? Was Nick around?"

"Mim is fine. Yes, Nick was nearby drinking Pickwick Ale and calling me a pup. I think he tries to get rid of me, but Mim doesn't let him."

"He doesn't want anyone around Mim, but himself. I think he drinks too much and maybe mistreats Mim, verbally."

Ruthie said, "How?"

"Well, he always says she's wrong. Haven't you heard him say, "You're wrong, Mim, you're wrong?"

"Oh, that, she doesn't pay any attention to him. Where's Beth?"

"She's upstairs supposedly doing her homework, but I heard music playing. Tell her to come down and set the table, please. I have some good news that I'll tell you at the table."

Ruthie headed to her bedroom. She wondered what the good news. Were they going to be able to live with their DAD, after all? Beth was flopped in the middle of the bed in a disarray of papers. Loud music was coming from a small radio on the nightstand.

"Emily wants you to go downstairs to set the table."

"Oh, yeah, well did you tell her it's your turn?"

"No, because it isn't."

"You always manage to get out of it. I suppose you buttered her up some way."

"I didn't, and you might as well know she's not very happy with the music. I hope you did your home work."

"You went to Mim's. I suppose you cried on her shoulder about Mary Calhoun. How much longer do we have to listen to that?"

Emily called, "Beth, please come down and set the table."

Beth answered very sweetly, "Okay, Emily, I'm on my way."

As she walked by Ruthie, she gave her a small shove. Ruthie said, "Can we go to see Dad after school tomorrow?"

"I guess so. I haven't been for awhile so that will work good." Ruthie figured Beth needed some money––Ruthie figured that was the reason she said, "That will work good."

"I want to tell him about Mary Calhoun."

"You know what, Ruthie? It's really getting stupid hearing that same old stuff."

"Well, my feelings were hurt, and I want to tell Dad about it."

"Oh, alright, but I hope this is the last time."

In the kitchen, Beth said, "Hey, Emily, I think it's Ruthie's turn to set the table. But, seeing she won't own up to it, I'll do it."

"Good, because it's your turn. Now, get started."

When the table was set, and they were seated in their places, Emily said, "I received some happy news today, and I wanted to tell you both. Harry is coming home from the Navy for good. He's very excited, and so am I."

Ruthie said, "Gosh, that's great. When?"

"In two weeks."

Beth said, "That's good news, especially for Ruthie. Now she can whine all over again about Mary Calhoun."

Emily said, "Beth, be nice. We'll be a family again."

Ruthie said, impulsively, "Emily is it okay if I go to see Dad after school tomorrow? I won't stay long."

"I guess so, but don't discuss it with me when you come home." When supper was over, Ruthie cleared the table. Beth was waiting in the kitchen. It was her turn to wash the dishes.

Ruthie put the dishes on the side of the sink. Beth stepped up close and said, "You are sooo two faced. That was great, 'Emily is it okay if I go see Dad?' I nearly choked. Now I suppose you don't need me to go with you."

"I didn't say that. You can still come."

"I'm not sure I want to."

"That's up to you, but I won't stop you."

"I'll tell you what, I'll let you know tomorrow."

The dishes were finished so Ruthie hung up the dishtowel and went upstairs.

On the way down the hall, Emily called out, "Ruthie, come here for a minute."

She was sitting near the dining room window again getting ready to knit.

Ruthie walked near to Emily's chair. "Emily did you want to talk to me?"

"Yes, I want to explain my feelings toward our father. I have the feeling that you think I am mean about him––that I blame him for Mama winding up in Medfield. I did. After much thought, I realize I could have done more to help her myself. I should have gone to Huff's Neck to see how you were."

She stopped, and Ruthie saw the tears rolling down her face. Ruthie was so stunned at this new behavior, she stood and stared with wide eyes. Then she heard her mother say, "We all do things we wish we could undo, but it's usually too late when we realize it."

Emily continued, "He didn't have to drink and forge checks. He only thought of himself. I am trying to forgive our father. I don't know if I ever will, completely, but I am working on it, so please be patient with me."

Ruthie chewed the edge of her finger then twisted a lock of hair with the same finger and said, "Okay, I will. Mama would be happy." Ruthie wanted to say, "She went without food so we could eat."

But instead she said, "Thank you, Emily." And left the dining room.

Beth was already in the bedroom lying on the bed when Ruthie entered.

Beth said, "I heard some of that talk between you and Emily. Do you believe her?" "Well, I'll have to wait and see. I hope she was being honest. I'll know more when I come back from seeing Dad tomorrow. I'm still a little worried. If she is really trying maybe she'll be interested in how he is. I'll give her a chance."

Beth said, "A chance, my foot. Giver her some rope, so she can hang herself. I don't think she's sorry."

Chapter 39

The next day after school, Ruthie met Beth at the bus stop so they could go to the antique shop to visit their father. On the bus, Ruthie said, "Are you going to ask for money, again?"

Beth shrugged her shoulders and said, "Well, I really didn't think about it, but now that you mention it, I will. You'll get some, too, because he won't give me any without offering you some. I know you won't say no."

Ruthie looked out the window and watched some leaves drift to the sidewalk. It made her think of the seagulls in Huff's Neck aimlessly flying over the water. She wished she were there to be with her mother, smell her powder and maybe walk through the marsh.

Beth poked her. "Ruthie, stop daydreaming. We are there."

Ruthie shook her head as if to shake the memories out. "Okay, okay."

When they stepped off the bus, the familiar slightly warm fall breeze blew as they walked up the steps to Mrs. Alexander's house. She answered the door. "Well, hello you two. Come in, come in, your father will be happy to see you. He was getting a little anxious not seeing you for a while."

Ruthie said, "Gee, we are sorry, but we had things going on in school, and the time passed so fast."

"Yeah, I sort of remember the times in my life at your age."

A big gray cat slept in the sun on the windowsill.

Beth said, "Wow, do you have a new cat? What is its name?"

"Sadie. She wandered into the yard and stayed. So I took her in."

"Gosh, I love cats. We had a cat named Penny a long time ago. Is your dog still here?"

"Oh, yes, he's here somewhere."

Tom came into the room and hugged both of the girls. Tom looked different; Ruthie didn't know what was different, maybe skinnier?

He said, "I thought I heard voices. I thought it was you two. That's great, I missed you."

Ruthie said, "Daddy, I have to talk to you about something that happened to me."

Beth look disgusted, as she said, "No, here it goes again, Ruthie just drop it."

Tom said, "No, I want to know what it is. If I can help, I want to."

Ruthie told the story of Mary Calhoun accusing her of being untrustworthy.

Tom listened carefully to every word and said, "Ruthie, people hurt each other too often. Lots of times, accusations are false. I am proud of you for going to Chuck to get to the root of the accusation. That's a good way to handle things. Did Emily help?"

"No, but Harry did. He's coming home from the Navy for good."

Beth said, "Yeah. Then Ruthie can whine to him anytime."

Tom said, "Beth, be nice."

"Well, that's all she does is talk about this Mary Calhoun. Kids hurt me. I stay away from them and forget about it."

"Beth, some people have that ability, Ruthie doesn't. Try to be more understanding."

Ruthie said, "I told Emily I was coming here today. She is trying to be nicer about you."

Beth said, "Don't believe that."

Ruthie told about the conversation she had had with Emily that Beth overheard.

Tom said, "I hope you're right Ruthie."

Then to Beth he admonished, "Let's give her a chance, okay?"

Mrs. Alexander brought some cookies and said, "Help yourself."

Ruthie munched on one and said, "Yum, my favorite." She took such a huge bite out of the chocolate chip cookie, half of it was gone.

The four of them sat in silence for a little while. Beth spoke first, "We have to go so Emily won't get upset and ruin her new feelings."

Tom said, "Now Beth, remember be nice."

They said their good byes as Tom gave them each a twenty-dollar bill.

Beth nudged Ruthie, "I knew you'd take it."

Mrs. Alexander walked to the sun porch with them and said, "Girls, I have to tell you something."

"What?" Ruthie asked?

"Your father hasn't been feeling well. I talked him into going to the doctor who said he has a serious blood disorder. Please come and see him more often.

Ruthie squeezed her hands together by her sides. "Gee, he's not going to die is he?"

"Well, it's in the early stages. If he takes care of himself, the doctor said he would be fine. He's not supposed to eat any spicy food or take drinks. So I hope he'll take the doctor's advice."

Ruthie's eyes began to water. She said, "I guess the three of us will never be able to live together. We just got back together. We'll come as often as we can."

Beth added, "Yes. We'll do that."

They said goodbye and Ruthie said, "Thank you for taking care of him."

She hugged Mrs. Alexander, went to the window and stroked Sadie. She thought he didn't seem sick, maybe the doctor was wrong.

They left in silence.

Chapter 40

When Ruthie and Beth arrived home, there was a strange Maroon Ford Coupe in the driveway. They walked up the back stairway. Ruthie said, "Wow, I hear voices, it's Harry, he's home." She grabbed Beth and gave her a squeeze.

Beth moved away slightly and said, "Big deal. Now you can tell him about *Mary Calhoun.*"

When they opened the kitchen door, Harry and Emily were at the kitchen table drinking coffee. Harry was dressed in his uniform. Emily smiled and squeezed his hand.

Ruthie said, "Hi, Harry, are you home for good? I hope so; we missed you, didn't we. Beth?"

She gave her a small nudge.

Beth said, "Yes, we really missed you. Is that your car?" The "we really missed you" sounded shaky like a wise remark.

"Yes, I'm home for good, and yes, that's my car."

Ruthie turned to Emily and said, "We went to see Daddy like we said, and Mrs. Alexander told us he's very sick."

"He is? Did she say what's wrong?"

"Something about not drinking or eating spicy foods. She told us to come and see him more often."

Beth said, "We felt sorry. He looked different, too. Kind of skinny."

"Well, that's too bad. I'll call Mrs. Alexander later. I'm going to start the supper. Actually it's all ready. I just have to reheat it. Ruthie you might as well go ahead and, set the table."

"Okay. What are we having?"

"Beef stew." Nobody responded. They didn't like it, but didn't dare say that. It tasted like thick, thick gravy with mixed vegetables in it. Harry said nothing; he must have hated it, too.

Ruthie set the table, and Beth went upstairs. On her way, she said over her shoulder, "It's nice your home, Harry."

"Thank you for that, Beth"

Ruthie set out four soup bowls, silverware, and a basket for rolls or crackers. She thought about her father and decided to go again to see him, maybe tomorrow.

Emily set a large flowered soup tureen in the middle of the table and brought some soft rolls, which she put in the breadbasket. Ruthie put glasses at each place for the usual milk or water.

The telephone rang as Emily returned to the kitchen. She stepped in the hall to answer it.

Ruthie heard her say, "Oh, hello Mrs. Alexander. I was going to call you." Her voice quivered. "Oh, no, when? Yes, yes, I'll come tomorrow. I'll come right now if you want. Thank you so much for everything. You've been most kind."

Ruthie leaned against the dining room wall. She heard Emily sniff.

Emily called Beth, Ruthie. When she reached the dining room, Emily said, "I have some sad news. Dad was refinishing a table for Mrs. Alexander in her back yard. She went to check on him and was not able to arouse him, he was lying on the ground. She called the doctor, but it was too late when he arrived. Dad had had a heart attack." Emily looked like she held back tears; she bit her lip, and, her color faded like the light gray top she was wearing.

Ruthie cried. "Now we have no mother or father. Maybe we should have gone to see him more." She rung her hands, "We should have gone more. We left him alone like what happened to mama."

Beth said, "Does this mean we are orphans? We don't have to go to an orphanage, do we?" Harry whispered, "No, you will stay with us, we want you here."

The phone rang again. This time it was Charlotte. Emily said, "Yes, we'll go tomorrow to make the plans. Yes they are sad, but holding up."

Ruthie wanted to go to Mim for comforting.

She asked Emily, "Is it alright if I go to Mim's ? I can't eat anything."

"Yes, and Beth can go to if she wants."

Emily said, "Ruthie, you and Beth have been good daughters. Please don't blame yourselves. Mama and Dad loved you, and they were proud of you. Just go see Mim."

Ruthie jumped up. "Thank you Emily. Come on Beth."

On the way to Mim's back gate, Ruthie said, "We should have been nicer to Dad. We acted like Emily and Charlotte did to Mama."

"No, we didn't. They did it on purpose. We did it because we went with our friends instead. Kids do that stuff."

They reached Mim's gate, her dog wagged his tail and walked to the back porch with them.

Nick answered the door in his tee shirt pulled over his belly, "Well, well, the pups, both of them. I suppose you want Mim?" The Pickwick Ale bottle was on the table. The place smelled like beer.

Ruthie said, "Yes, is it alright?"

"What if I said no? Aw, it's alright. Mim, it's the pups, both of them." Nick burped, loudly.

Mim came into the kitchen in her navy robe and white fluffy slippers. She said, "Beth and Ruthie, how nice, come in." She had a white ring around her mouth from eating Tums.

They went to their spots in the living room. A dish of chocolates was on the table. Mim said, "Have some candy. I ate too much, and it gave me indigestion."

Ruthie burst into tears. "Mim, we are awful like Emily and Charlotte. We didn't go to see Daddy very much. Now he's dead."

Beth said, "He wanted us to come more, and we didn't."

Mim went to the small couch and squeezed in between them. She wrapped her arms around them. "I'll help you through this. I am so sorry. When did it happen?"

"Today, after we left. He was finishing a table for Mrs. Alexander. She found him. He died from a heart attack."

What did Emily say?"

Ruthie said, "She was nice about it. She let us come over here. She didn't even make us eat. We couldn't we were too sad."

Beth said, "Yeah, it's a good thing, yuck beef stew. Harry's home. He gets on her. We're orphans now, but he said we could live there and not go to an orphanage."

Mim said, "That's the way it should be. He's a good man."

"Yeah, I hope he means it."

Ruthie said, "Mim, will you help us to go to the funeral? Can we go with you? We don't want to sneak like we did at Mama's."

"I said I'd help you through this, and I will, beginning with the funeral."

"Are those pups still here?" was heard from the kitchen.

"Yes, they are. Their father died today, and I am trying to comfort them."

"They run to you with every problem."

Mim said, "Oh, Nick, you aren't jealous, I hope."

Ruthie said, "Maybe we should go."

"Don't listen to that. He likes all the attention. Stay as long as you wish."

But Beth said, "No, we should go. We don't want him to be upset. Come on, Ruthie."

Mim finally agreed and walked with them to the back door.

Nick was in the kitchen with a nearly empty bottle of ale. As they walked through, he said, "Girls, you pups, you can come anytime. I can be your father. Try not to be sad."

Ruthie stepped up to him, took his hand and squeezed it. She took Beth by the arm and they left. Over their shoulders, they said, "Bye, Mim."

Beth added, "We love you. Remember the funeral."

Chapter 41

As they walked through Mim's yard back to their house, Ruthie said, "Gee, do you think we can actually go to the funeral?"

Beth said, "Yup, even if we have to sneak. I think Mim will fix it for us to go. Did you notice that Nick was actually friendly? I think he does like us to visit."

"Yeah, he pretends a lot. Do you think Mim will call Emily? I wonder if she'll be upset. Remember, she said not to discuss anything with the neighbors."

"Yeah, but this is different, and Mim is more than a neighbor. She's our pretend grandmother."

They approached the stairs to their kitchen, Ruthie said, "Here goes the seventh degree questioning."

"Yeah, half the time I don't even listen."

They entered the kitchen and heard voices in the living room. Harry and Emily were talking in low voices and soft music was playing, Bing Crosby singing "The Lonesome Road."

Ruthie and Beth walked into the living area, even though Ruthie felt they were intruding she said, "Mim said we can go to the funeral with her, is that alright?"

"No, it would be nicer if we all go as a family. Charlotte and I decided to make it a private funeral with just a few close friends outside the family."

Beth said, "We already asked Mim if we could go with her, and she said it would be fine."

Emily said, "You didn't do anything wrong, but it's better if we go as a family. You can tell Mim and Nick. They'll understand. We are having a blanket of roses over his casket that says, "Father."

"Okay. We'll let Mim know."

Ruthie asked, "Is he going to be buried where Mama is?"

"Yes, beside her."

Harry said, "You will feel better surrounded with a lot of family who care, too."

"Okay. I think Daddy would have liked that, anyway.

She and Beth said goodnight and left to go to their room.

Ruthie began to weep as she went up the stairs. Beth took her hand, squeezed it and said, "We'll be alright. Harry is here and he makes things better."

When they reached their room, the lamp was on, and a small bouquet of purple asters was on the table beside it.

Beth said, "Gee, maybe I'm wrong about Emily. She must have done this."

Ruthie sniffed and said, "Gosh, it's nice. Maybe she does like us here after all."

Beth said, "Hey, I have an idea, lets call the Mckinnels and tell them what happened. Maybe they would want to come to the funeral. I bet they would."

"Yeah, it'll be nice to see them again, even if it is sad. We can catch up on things. Mrs. McKinnel would want to know if we are happy. I guess we should ask Emily. It's your idea, you can do the asking."

"Okay, tomorrow."

"No, go down now, and see if we can. Emily seems to be on our side."

Beth left the bedroom. Ruthie waited at the top of the stairs to hear the conversation.

Beth was in the living room pretty fast, Ruthie heard, "Emily, is it alright if we call the Mckinnels to tell them about Dad?"

There was a slight pause in the conversation, and then Ruthie heard, "Yes, as a matter of fact, Harry and I were talking about that. You can do it in the morning."

"Gosh, thank you, that will be good."

When Beth was on the top step, Ruthie said, "I heard. Good. It will make everything seem easier."

Chapter 42

The next morning was cold and looked dreary. Ruthie looked out the window and thought the weather matched her feelings. She poked Beth who was curled up with her hands tucked under her cheek still sound asleep. Ruthie wished she could trade places. Get up, we have to call the Mckinnels. Maybe we'll sneak to the funeral home like we did for Mama"

Beth sat up, yawned, rubbed her eyes and said, "Huh? Go the funeral home, why?"

"We want to make sure it is Daddy there."

"Huh, why wouldn't he be there?"

"I have a funny feeling, and I want to talk to that man who helped with Mama."

"I'm not sure, but okay after we call the Mckinnels."

"What if Emily catches us? She's beginning to act nicer."

"We'll deal with that if it happens."

They went to the kitchen where Emily was alone at the table drinking coffee. She was still wearing her bathrobe.

She said, "I hope you were able to sleep."

Beth and Ruthie assured her they had. "First we talked about Daddy, and then we must have fallen asleep."

Ruthie said, "Can we go to Mim's, and tell her we will be going to the funeral as a family?"

"That will be fine. There's oatmeal and a pot of cocoa. Eat your breakfast, and then you can call the McKinnels and go to Mim's."

Beth looked at Ruthie, made a face about the oatmeal, usually luke warm and lumpy. Ruthie raised her eyebrows, but said nothing, even though it was always terrible.

Beth said, "Is it okay if I just have toast and juice?'

Emily said, "Yes."

Ruthie said, "I want that, too."

"Okay. Eat what you want, and then clean up afterward."

"We will,"

Emily left the kitchen.

Ruthie said, "Gee, you have nerve."

"I noticed you took me up on it."

"Shut up. You always make me do the dirty work."

"I just decided I don't want you to go the funeral home after all."

"Try and stop me."

Emily came in to the kitchen, "Who is going to the funeral home?"

Ruthie quickly said, "Oh we were talking about all of us going and how nice it will be."

Emily headed to the bathroom.

Beth said, "What was that about nerve?"

"Shut up and eat."

When they finished and cleaned up the breakfast dishes, they headed to the phone to call the McKinnels.

Ruthie made the call. "Hi, Mrs. Mckinnel, this is Ruthie."

"Gosh, how nice, how are you?"

"Well, I have some sad news." She started to cry.

Mrs. Mckinnel said, "What is it dear? Can I help?"

"Daddy died from a heart attack. I wanted you to know. Can you come to the funeral tomorrow?"

"Of, course I will, dear. Is it at Russell's funeral home?"

"Yes, eleven o'clock. Thank you. Beth and I can't wait to see you. We miss you."

"We'll be there. I'll bring Jane and Sonny."

"We'll sit together. See you tomorrow. We love you. Bye."

"I love you, too. Bye."

Beth said, "You can really turn it on."

"Why didn't you do it, then?"

They headed upstairs to get dressed.

It was about ten o'clock when they yelled to Emily, "We are going to Mim's."

"Okay."

Outside in the gloomy morning, a light mist fell as they headed to Mim's.

Nick answered the door, tee shirt, but no beer smell. "The pups. You want Mim, huh?"

"If it's okay."

Mim called, "Nick, who is it?"

"The pups."

"Send them in the living room."

Beth and Ruthie headed there to the usual place.

Mim was dressed in her nurses uniform. She said, "Good morning, I hope you both are feeling better."

Ruthie said, "Hi, Mim. We have something to tell you."

Beth interrupted, "We can't go the funeral with you and Nick. Emily won't let us. She's jealous."

"That's not true. She thinks we should go as a family. Beth is making that up."

"I understand that. We'll be together as friends and family. Your father would have liked that. I hate to rush, but I have to work for awhile today."

They hugged her and left through the kitchen. Nick was already pouring some Pickwick Ale."

Beth said, "Early start, huh?"

"You pup, it has nothing to do with you."

Ruthie said, "She is too fresh."

They went to the back door to go home, but instead headed to the street going to the funeral home.

Ruthie said, "Beth, don't do that, Nick might not let us see Mim."

"Oh, okay, but he drinks too much beer."

"It's not our business. Try to ignore it."

They walked toward Hancock Street to the funeral home. Ruthie said, "I hope that man is there."

"He probably will be."

They reached the front door of the funeral home. The glass in the door was clear like it had just been cleaned. The gold letters, Russell Funeral Home shone like new. The man in the gray suit was there and greeted them like they wanted. "I hoped to see you again, but not this way." He was just as nice as before. Inside soft couches were placed for visitor's comfort. Ruthie shivered as she wondered why anyone would want to sit near dead people unless was someone they loved.

Beth said, "Can we see our Dad?"

"You know I'm not supposed to, but I'll make another exception. This way."

They walked behind him a place in the corner of the next room. Ruthie thought it was the same spot where their mother had been. A large fake palm tree was close to the window.

She cried loudly as she ran towards the casket. "Daddy, Daddy, we should have been nicer." She looked at her Dad, lying so still with his hair combed neatly and no paint or varnish smell. Even his fingernails were clean. She said, "Daddy, we are here, Beth and me, we miss you."

The man took Ruthie's hand and reached for Beth's. He said, "I didn't know your Dad, but I have a daughter, and I would be happy if she cared about me the way you care. Things will work out, they have a way of doing that, especially when you don't think it's possible. Time takes care of that."

Beth and Ruthie leaned against him. Ruthie said, "Please don't tell anyone we came here."

She took Beth's hand and turned to go.

The man said, "I won't say anything about your being here." They thanked him and left quickly so Emily wouldn't question where they had been.

The sun had broken the mist creating a mild temperature. They headed home in silence. Ruthie thought about Beth telling Harry that they were orphans. It was strange; she thought orphans were other people, not them.

Chapter 43

The funeral was to be held at eleven o'clock. Emily awakened Ruthie and Beth at eight o'clock.

Ruthie got of bed, walked to the window took a look at the clear sky and thought about her mother. It was the first time since her mother's death that she was glad her mother wasn't here. She didn't need any more sadness. Ruthie thought about Beth saying now they are orphans. She didn't feel like an orphan. Was it because Harry had tried to reassure them they would always be living with he and Emily? What made her insecure? Was she always going to feel that way?

Beth disturbed her reverie. "Hey, Ruthie I think I'll wear my gray skirt instead of my navy. I don't want to be dressed like you."

"I don't care. I'm glad. People will probably be sad for us so I suppose it doesn't matter. Gee, I hope people don't feel sorry for us from now on."

"I hope we don't have to eat that luke warm lumpy oatmeal."

Emily called, "Ruthie, Beth, come and eat your breakfast."

Beth said, "Yuck, I can't wait."

They walked into the kitchen and there was Harry cooking French toast. They could smell the crusty bread cooking. Orange juice was already on the table. Beth said, "Wow, that smells great. I'm glad we aren't having lumpy oatmeal." Harry was at the stove dressed in a blue shirt and gray slacks. They looked like his suit slacks. His wavy brown hair was neatly combed. There was a small pile of French Toast in one corner of the pan.

The syrup was heating in a small saucepan.

Ruthie shot a warning look to her. She changed the subject.

"Harry, is it okay if I sit with you at the funeral home?"

"Sure. I'll tell you what you, Ruthie and I will sit together."

Ruthie said, "That's sounds like a good idea."

"To me, too," Beth said.

Emily came into the kitchen dressed in a black silk dress and black stockings. Her hair was thin and mousy but she had it tied back in a way that was becoming. She said, "You two should start thinking about getting dressed."

Ruthie said, "I'm not hungry. I just ate a small piece of the French toast. Thank you, Harry."

She spoke over her shoulder as she headed upstairs.

She walked to the closet, rifled through it and found her navy skirt. Emily had ironed her white shirt and pinned a navy grosgrain bow near the neckline. She had black leather low-heeled shoes to wear.

Beth ambled into the room and headed for the closet. She said, "Emily ironed my shirt."

"She ironed mine, too. I guess she feels sorry for us."

"I wouldn't go that far."

Around ten thirty, they got into Harry's car, Emily and Harry in front and Ruthie and Beth in the back. There was very little conversation on the way to the funeral home, which was only about ten minutes away.

The funeral home had sparkling glass in the doors. A basket of flowers on legs was in side the entrance with a card that read from Mim and Nick.

Emily, Harry, Beth and Ruthie went in together. Mim, Nick, and Charlotte were sitting together talking, softly. Mim came towards Beth and Ruthie and hugged them.

The minister glanced around and when he was sure everyone was there, he began speaking. He mentioned how time has a way of being a great healer and though we want to remember Tom, we eventually learn to live with the loss. He said a prayer and then everyone headed to the cars to the cemetery.

The casket with the blanket of roses that read father was moved to the hearse and along with the flowers from Nick and Mim.

At the grave the minister read from the Bible. At the end, Charlotte and Emily planned where everyone could meet for lunch, the had decided on the Fox and Hounds near the cemetery.

Beth and Ruthie stayed close to each other as they headed to the grill.

Ruthie whispered, "I keep remembering that you said 'we are orphans'"

Chapter 44

The next day, Ruthie met Mary Ann at the end of Mary Ann's driveway. Ruthie scuffed along instead of being her usual bubbly self.

Mary said, "Gosh, I am sorry about your Dad, just when you were getting close to him again.

Are you going to be staying here with Emily and Harry?"

"Yes, see Beth mentioned being orphans, but Harry mentioned there would be no move. We can stay with them. It was good; because even Emily was happy to tell us it was fine. I'm not sure she means it, but for now it's working."

Wow, what a relief. I was afraid you'd have to move."

"Guess who called me? Frank. He was so nice telling me he was sorry and everything."

Mary Ann said, "Gosh, I wonder how Mary Calhoun will act. Maybe we won't see her." They passed the stadium right on time. Only ten minutes and they would be in the schoolyard.

When they arrived at the side door o the school building, Mary Ann said, "Don't look now, but it's Mary coming towards us."

Mary stepped closer and said, "Gee, Ruthie, I feel sorry about your father. You'll probably have to move, huh?"

"No, my sister and I are staying where we are."

"Oh? Somebody said you'd be moving to the state home over by the police department."

Mary Ann said, "That's pretty mean if you ask me."

"Nobody asked you. I did hear that this morning."

"Well, you're pathetic saying something like that after a person's father died. Come on Ruthie, we should get away from here, anyway before the bell rings."

Ruthie turned away and walked towards her homeroom, tears streamed down her cheeks.

She passed Frank in the hall. He said, "Hi firecracker."

Ruthie turned her face, but he continued, "Firecracker, what's up?"

MaryAnn said, "Mary Calhoun again. She just said something hateful."

Frank stepped closer to Ruthie, grabbed her hand and said, "Come on, don't let her get to you." He held her hand and playfully swung it around. "That's what she likes. She wins when you do that. Lighten up." He continued to swing her hand.

Ruthie looked at his smile and couldn't help but return it.

The bell rang so they had to go the their home room classes. She called out, "See you later."

He said, "After school."

Chapter 45

When Ruthie entered the eleventh grade at Quincy High, Emily became a friend; something Ruthie never thought would happen. At times, Ruthie felt she could almost confide in her, like when she became attracted to Joe in her Latin class.

Just before her senior year she spent most of her days at the baseball field in West Quincy. It was a small field, dusty with bleachers at the infield and some along the side near first base and the others near third base where Ruthie sat. All of the benches were painted dark green and were filled with splinters in some spots. It wasn't easy wearing shorts.

The reason Ruthie was there was she had been smitten in her Latin class by a dark brown haired six-footer, a third baseman called Joe. Ruthie walked to the field every day. It was no small trek around three miles one-way. But when she thought of Joe at the other end, it was worth every step even on the humid days.

After the game, he would shag flies with his friends, but before he did that, he'd come over, say goodbye and "See you tomorrow." Ruthie was so thrilled she could hardly breathe.

One Tuesday after the game he came over to the bleachers and said, "Hey, wear your bathing suit tomorrow. We're going to the quarry to swim. On Wednesdays, it's lady's day and all the guys wear suits."

"I'll try, but Emily probably won't let me. I am having some trouble since I painted your name on my leg." She remembered the scene earlier in the day when Emily discovered she had painted Joe in clear nail polish on her thigh. When she removed it, the letters were white against the tan around it. It was quite obvious. Emily screamed, "That's cheap. It's bad enough you chase him every day there's a practice or a game. I want you to stop it."

"I thought it was cute and that he'd like it. I didn't realize it was cheap."

"Well, let it get tanned and don't do it again."

Maybe that was a way to get of going to the quarry, Ruthie was afraid of it anyhow. She had heard about the sharp pointed granite where the kids dove into the water. There was no other way to get to the water except to dive.

Joe said, "It figures, but she'll get over it. Bye." Ruthie wanted to lean against him but all she managed was to brush up close then some of his teammates were waiting and calling him so he left in a hurry.

Ruthie's heart felt like it showed through her tee shirt it raced so fast. She yelled after him, "I may have to come without my bathing suit. Is that ok?" But, he didn't hear.

On the way home, she ran into, Tommy, Joe's brother. Tommy was tall, but his hair was a sandy blonde and he had the same blue eyes as Joe.

He called, "Hey, Ruthie can I walk with you? I'm going down near your house."

"Sure. How come?"

"I'm going to the beach with some kids who live near you. I hope the tide's in."

"I think it is. I don't check it as much since I have been going to O'Rourke Field."

"Yeah, I heard you go there a lot."

"Who told you?"

"I forget, but I think it was one of the girls, maybe Donna Johnson. She told somebody she liked Joe, but Joe doesn't care about her, he likes you."

"Really? So you think he doesn't mind if I go to the field?"

"No, I think he waits for you. Well, bye here's the road to my friend's house."

"Bye. Thanks for walking with me."

Ruthie turned to ask if Joe mentioned her name, but Tommy was gone.

It was getting late towards suppertime. She hoped she was on time. She could hear Emily saying, "You can't go to that field for awhile."

She wanted to tell Emily she thought she loved Joe, but she didn't dare. She said to herself, "I wonder if Mama would talk to me about it."

It was bad enough to hear Beth's reaction, "Oh now you're in love, first it was the Calhoun kid we heard about all the time, now it's this. I hope you get over it fast. Or we could call your life, "As Ruthie's World Turns."

Ruthie said, "Just shut up. Nobody is begging you to listen. Most of the time you're eaves dropping, anyway."

Emily called from the kitchen, "That's enough you two."

Beth continued, "Oh, Ruthie is in love. The summer of love. Aren't we lucky?"

Chapter 46

Ruthie's summer of love turned to fall and back to Quincy High in the twelfth grade. She was thrilled to be at the end of Quincy High even though it would meant no more walks with Marianne, her ace confidante, in the mornings. They had talked of college, but no decisions had been made. Actually Ruthie and Marianne talked about working first, but they hadn't really decided on that, either, nor did they have any idea at what. Ruthie had thought she'd like to go to a two-year business school in Boston, but she hadn't mentioned it to anyone. She always wanted to be someone's private secretary ever since she had helped in the Quincy High office and watched the school secretary.

The first day of school, Ruthie met Marianne at the end of the driveway. Ruthie was dressed in a pink sweater and a dark gray straight skirt. Marianne had a dark brown skirt on topped with a white sweater. The weather was clear, a mild autumn day. Ruthie said, "Gosh, isn't it perfect today? And here we are in our last year."

"Yeah, I'm a little nervous, I don't know why. I guess I am wondering what graduation will bring."

"Yeah, Joe said he is joining the Navy. In a way I wish everything could stay as it is. You know, with Joe. I'll never meet anyone like him."

"How does Emily feel about that?"

"She despises him because he's a Catholic and lives in West Quincy, you know the wrong side of the tracks thing again. I think she's glad he's going in the Navy."

"I wonder how she got like that"

"Who knows, if it weren't that, it would be something else."

Marianne said, "Gosh, we're at school already. That was the quickest walk, ever. There's Frank coming towards us. He looks sharp as usual."

He hollered, "Hey, you two, what's up? How was your summer?"

Ruthie said, "It was wonderful. I spent most of it at O'Rourke Field."

Frank said, "Near third base?" Then he laughed.

Ruthie laughed and said, "Pretty close."

Ruthie thought she was lucky to be able to keep Frank for a friend even after she became interested in Joe. Their relationship was smooth.

Marianne said, "I spent mine at Gunrock, my family's cottage."

Marie Calhoun, dressed perfectly in a navy skirt with a yellow angora sweater, and not a hair was out of place walked up behind Frank.

Marianne whispered, "Not again."

Marie said, "Hi, Ruthie, you never give up, do you? How does the baseball star, Joe, feel about you still making a play for Frank?"

Nobody responded.

Instead, Frank said, "Gee, it's our last year here. Seems weird we won't be coming here anymore. Yeah, I had a good summer down the Cape."

Ruthie said, "The Cape is always great." A loud bell rang signaling time to get to homeroom. "Saved by the bell."

Turning to Marianne, she said, "See you at lunch."

Marianne said, "Okay, let's get out of here."

Marie said in a sing song tone, "Bye, Ruthie."

Ruthie felt proud of herself that she had taken Frank's advice from the past and ignored Marie, even though it didn't change Marie's snide remarks.

All of them moved towards their homerooms. The hall was crowded and noisy as they weaved their way. They had the same assignments as the previous year.

As Ruthie walked towards Miss Cash's room, she felt proud of herself that she had taken Frank's advice from the past and ignored Marie.

Then she thought about Latin class and Joe and quivered a little.

She was near failing in Latin, and Miss Clark, her teacher, had warned her if she failed she would not graduate. Ruthie didn't really have the conjugations learned as well as necessary. They bored her and she continued to think about Joe, instead.

Chapter 47

Ruthie arrived at Miss Clark's room just before the first period; she knocked, Miss Clark said, "Come in."

The shades were pulled half way down to block the early morning sun making the room feel cozy. Ruthie took that as a positive sign, sometimes the room seemed cold. She cleared her throat twice and fiddled with a lock of her hair as she walked towards Miss Clark sitting at her desk, which was covered with books and papers. She was dressed in the green silk jersey print dress with the dirty belt. Ruthie figured she had her dresses cleaned but forgot the belts, because all of her belts were dirty.

Miss Clark said I am glad to see you, Ruthie, I hope you are here about your grades.

"Yes, I am."

"Right now, as you know, you are barely passing with a very low C bordering on a high D. Do you have any plans on how to improve your grade? You would have to repeat the twelfth grade if you don't pass. If you do that, you'd still be stuck in the same grade you have now."

"My plan is to come for extra help after school if you let me?" Ruthie shrugged her shoulders and rocked her knees. "Whatever you suggest is what I will do."

"Yes, that's possible. You need to put in some effort like learning to memorize the conjugations: i, isti, it, imus, istus, erunt. You'll have to review, review."

"I can do it, because I want to do it. I will try to do better, honest. May I come after school if I have questions about the tenses? Can you give me the list I should memorize?"

"Yes, I have it right here. Just let me know what days, and we will work out a plan." Miss Clark handed Ruthie a bunch of papers.

"I have set a goal for myself. I want to try for at least a B."

"That's wonderful, Ruthie, but I think you are going a little overboard. Going from failing to a B sounds ambitious, but it's good to challenge yourself. I will help anyway I can. You will have to pass every test from now on. Not all of it is memorization. It includes writing a paragraph."

"I can do it with your help, thank you, Miss Clark." Ruthie left the classroom. Ruthie thought Miss Clark was nice and very fair. Ruthie turned to the papers Miss Clark had given her, rifled through them and decided it was a lot of work. Why did she let it go this far? She thought she could bluff her way, but Latin was not easy. Could she memorize all that stuff? She made up her mind yes was the only answer. If she flunked, she'd have to listen to Emily nagging her, making fun of her and the fact she picked Latin as a course to begin with. Emily wouldn't let up and she'd probably be kept away from Joe, more than now.

She looked at the pile of papers from Miss Clark and figured she might have to start at the very first chapter and that she would be studying in the wee small hours. She would have to bribe Beth if she said I, isti, it, imus, istis, erunt in her sleep. Beth told Emily Ruthie was talking Latin in her sleep keeping her awake. That's the end of her new pink sweater. She felt defeated already.

Ruthie decided to go to the study hall to do the studying.

The corridor was nearly empty, except for a student or two, Marie Calhoun was one of them. Ruthie glanced up.

Marie, dressed to the nines, in a matching pink sweater, socks and skirt said, "Hey, Ruthie, are you having trouble in Latin? I heard you might not pass. Gee, that would keep you from graduating, wouldn't it?"

"Yes, but I am getting extra help, and I think it will turn out good."

"How does that work? Do you repeat the twelfth grade when you flunk?"

"I don't know, because I get A's and B's, as a rule. Not everyone gets A's in Latin, it's really hard. I have to go, bye."

"Oh, yeah, it's sooooo hard." Marie was an A student in Latin and French.

When she walked away, she yelled, "Good luck Ruthie, I hope you make it. If you don't, you could get kicked out of cheerleading. Too bad if that happened."

Ruthie kept walking towards the study hall. She wanted to argue with Marie, but she knew it wouldn't do any good.

She tried not to worry when she thought of getting a B in Latin, but she nervously bit her fingernail even though most of it was memorizing. Anybody could do that. Maybe she could work with Joe. He was passing, but only with a C. Gee, could they both improve their grades? And be with each other as they did it. Nah, that won't work, she needed to push herself. She couldn't do that with Joe there. She had to be positive and make herself interested in Latin. She bit her another nail when she thought of getting kicked off the cheerleading squad. Emily would say, "I knew this would come to no good end. Now you're flunking."

Maybe she could talk to the study hall teacher and find out the best way to get into good study habits. It worked for Marianne when she had problems in math.

Ruthie put her books down as she entered the study hall before she spoke to Mr. Phillips. Mr. Phillips had a round stomach where a long tie usually hung near his belt. He looked stern with his tiny wire glasses hanging down his nose.

When he looked up, he said, "Yes Ruthie, do you need help?"

"Yes, I was wondering if you could show me the best way to study some Latin?"

"Are you behind?"

"Yes, pretty far, and I could fail."

"I had heard that and was very surprised because you are a good student. Maybe another student could help. I happen to know Marie Calhoun excels in Latin. She comes in here often. Maybe she'd be glad to help you."

Ruthie thought she would throw up as her stomach churned. She said, "Uh, well, we don't get along too well. Marie doesn't like me."

"Gee, Ruthie, I thought everyone liked you."

"Yeah, well Marie doesn't. Studying with her won't work."

"Hmm. I'll dig out a book or two that teaches study habits. I might have one that concentrates on foreign languages. Will that work? I think the Marie Calhoun suggestion is the best. Maybe another student could help, I'll see what I can do."

Ruthie needed the help. How could she work with Marie? What if Marie deliberately tried to confuse her?

Ruthie looked at Mr. Phillips and said softly, "I'd like to try the books. Thank you, Mr. Phillips. I'll be here a lot

Chapter 48

Ruthie went to the study hall for the first time. She dreaded and scared of what was coming. It was sunny near the windows where the shades were drawn to block the glare. Mr. Phillips, wearing his long skinny tie and wire glasses said, "Ruthie, may I see you after you get your books organized?"

Ruthie put her books and study papers on a desk and stepped towards Mr. Phillips. He said, "I found some information on studying foreign languages, specifically Latin for you." He handed her two books.

She said, "Wow, this is great, thank you."

"And, I found a student who will work with you, too. Jim Keelon, do you know him?"

Ruthie knew him and knew him to be stuck on himself, but she said, "When am I supposed to meet him?"

"Oh, he'll be here in a little while."

Ruthie pretended to be glad, but she didn't want to work with him, because he was a "hail fellow well met," type. "Okay, Mr. Phillips. I hope it wasn't too much trouble."

"Not at all. I hope it works out for you, Ruthie."

Ruthie headed back to the desk where she had laid her things.

The door to the study hall opened and in walked Jim Keelon, all cocky six feet of him. Not a hair was out of place. He was wearing gray slacks, a black sweater over a white shirt that had the collar opened. It was rumored he was being voted class Adonis.

He said, condescendingly, "Hi, Ruthie, I hear you need some help with Latin. That should be easy. How far behind are you?" He emphasized "far."

Ruthie answered, "Hi, Jim, way behind, thanks for coming."

He said, "Where shall we start?"

"Conjugations of the tenses and practice writing paragraphs."

"Ohhhh, is that all? That should be a cinch. I brought a book of mine that helped me a lot."

The door opened, and in walked Marie Calhoun in a beautiful pink sweater and matching skirt. Her hair was perfect. She walked to the desk where Ruthie and Jim were sitting and said audibly with a loud laugh, "Ruthie, you never quit, do you?"

Ruthie shrugged her shoulders and said, "I think I'm in for it."

Jim whispered, "We've been dating."

Ruthie said, "I don't know what you mean. I am trying to catch up on my Latin."

Jim is helping me."

"Sure, just like Frank was just a friend. What happened to Joe, couldn't get to third base?"

At that point, Mr. Phillips walked up and said to Marie, "Are you here to study? If not, please don't disturb those who are. "Please leave if you aren't studying."

Marie meekly turned to leave, but said over her shoulder, "Jim, don't forget our date Friday night, seven o'clock."

He said, "Yeah, okay."

Ruthie turned to Jim and said, "Boy, I'm in for it from her."

"Aw, don't worry about it, everybody knows she's trouble. I've taken her out a little bit."

"Well, she accused me of trying to take Frank away from her."

"She's does that to cover up when a guy gives her the brush."

They went back to studying. Jim taught her some easy ways to remember the tenses, and it worked out very well.

Ruthie thanked him, borrowed the book he brought and agreed to meet the next afternoon after school.

He said, "Don't worry about Marie. You'll probably hear from her, but don't give her any satisfaction."

Ruthie said, "Okay, I'll try, see you tomorrow. To herself, she said, "Gee, he's nice. I can't wait 'till tomorrow."

On her way out, she stopped by to thank Mr. Phillips and told him, "I think this is going to work out, thank you for taking your time to help me."

He said, "You're a good student and I'd like to see that continue."

"It will. I'll be back tomorrow, bye."

"Good, bye."

As Ruthie walked toward the door, she looked but Jim was gone. He was nice and not at all stuck on himself. He was tall and his eyes sparkled when he Ch 49

The next morning, Ruthie was up at six forty-five. She woke Beth by shaking her and saying, "Beth, get up, I have to talk to you."

Beth said, "Sto-op, I'm tired."

"Sit up, just for a minute, it's important."

"Wha-at?"

"Can I borrow your royal blue sweater? I am meeting someone this afternoon."

"I bet, probably at the baseball field. You can. Don't get it dirty."

"Thanks, I'll make it up to you."

"Oh, sure, I won't hold my breath."

Ruthie was elated, she decided to wear it with her light gray skirt. She went to the bathroom to bathe and wash her hair. She wanted to look perfect when she went to the study hall to meet Jim.

She thought of Joe and the baseball field and mumbled to herself, "Who cares, he's always busy with sports anyway." She decided to go to Marianne's house instead of waiting for her that way they could get an early start, and she could tell Marianne all the latest news.

Emily was in the kitchen wearing her plaid bathrobe drinking coffee at the kitchen table. She said to Ruthie, "This is a surprise, up so early and wearing Beth's new sweater, did she say it was okay?"

"Yes, and I have to be in school a little early. I am getting extra help in Latin."

"Oh, yes that's right. I nearly forgot. The foreign language student."

Ruthie ignored the sarcasm, gulped some orange juice and a piece of toast and said on her way out the kitchen door, "Bye, I'm on my way to meet Marianne."

"Alright, I'll be glad when the study hall thing is over with. Bye."

Ruthie rushed down the drive towards the big tree at the end, blowing gently in the morning breeze, crossed the street and hurried up on Marianne's porch which was littered with dog things, a bed, toys, and bowl, rang the bell, her brother, Frank, answered the door. "Wow, you're early. Marianne, Ruthie is here."

"Okay, coming."

Frank said, "Come on in."

Ruthie stepped into a tiny hall at the foot of a stairway as Marianne came down the stairs looking disheveled. Her hair looked quickly combed and her lipstick looked crooked. "Gosh, I'm a mess. You are really early, what's the rush?"

"I have a lot to tell you, and I can't wait."

They got outside on the sidewalk and headed toward Hancock Street. "Marianne, I don't think I care much about Joe anymore. Remember when I mentioned I was flunking Latin and I didn't know what to do? Well, Miss Clark set it up with Mr. Phillips for me to go to the study hall for extra study. Mr. Phillips arranged for Jim Keelon to help me. I have flipped out over him. He's not the person people think he is. He is very good looking, is very smart and has a great sense of caring about other people."

Marianne said, "Hold on. How many times has he helped you?"

"Twice."

"Oh, twice, that's really getting to know someone, he acts stuck on himself. You know like talking maybe a total of twenty minutes in a study hall. Give me a break."

"I know it sounds crazy, especially since he has been dating Marie Calhoun."

"Oh, that's perfect. You don't need the headache from her again. Emily is going to flip, another Catholic boy. You're asking for it, this time. Last week nobody could match Joe. He was the best third baseman, handsome, tall and had the best personality, wow what a change."

They reached the halfway mark towards school, the stadium.

Ruthie said, "I know it's a complete change, but it's a feeling I have, Jim is soft spoken, polite, handsome and nice, I'm convinced, what else can I say?"

They reached the schoolyard. Marianne said, "You don't have to say anything. Here comes Marie and behind her is the man of the hour, Jim. This should set the day off good."

Marie stepped closer and said, "Well if it isn't the Latin student and man chaser."

Ruthie said, "It's not what you think, I have to pass Latin and I am desperate for the extra help."

"You're desperate all right, but not the way you're pretending. First it was Frank, then Joe, and now it's Jim. You're getting boy crazy."

Jim stepped closer and said, "Hi everyone." He was wearing black slacks, a blue checked shirt and a light gray jacket. Ruthie's heart jumped a little.

He said to Ruthie, "Wow that color looks good on you. Don't forget the study hall later."

"Thanks, I won't. I worked on what we talked about so I'm getting caught up."

Marie interrupted, "Jim, remember Friday. Is it still on?"

"I'm not sure. I might not be able to get the car."

Marie said, "You're last in line, Frank, then Joe and now you. Doesn't that bother you? Good luck."

Then the bell for first class rang. Everyone began to scatter. Marie was the first to run.

Marianne said, "Isn't she pathetic? Look at her run. Saved again by the bell."

Chapter 49

The next morning, Ruthie was up at six forty-five. She woke Beth by shaking her and saying, "Beth, get up, I have to talk to you."

Beth said, "Sto-op, I'm tired."

"Sit up, just for a minute, it's important." Beth had her pillow rolled in a ball. Her hair had two curlers in it in front, and the rest was loose. She yawned.

"Wha-at?"

"Can I borrow your royal blue sweater? I am meeting someone this afternoon."

"I bet, probably at the baseball field. You can. Don't get it dirty."

"Thanks, I'll make it up to you."

"Oh, sure, I won't hold my breath."

Ruthie was elated, she decided to wear it with her light gray skirt. She went to the bathroom to bathe and wash her hair. She wanted to look perfect when she went to the study hall to meet Jim.

She thought of Joe and the baseball field and mumbled to herself, "Who cares, he's always busy with sports anyway." She decided to go to Marianne's house instead of waiting for her that way they could get an early start, and she could tell Marianne all the latest news.

Emily was in the kitchen wearing her plaid bathrobe drinking coffee at the kitchen table. She said to Ruthie, "This is a surprise, up so early and wearing Beth's new sweater, did she say it was okay?"

"Yes, and I have to be in school a little early. I am getting extra help in Latin."

"Oh, yes that's right. I nearly forgot. The foreign language student."

Ruthie ignored the sarcasm, gulped some orange juice and a piece of toast and said on her way out the kitchen door, "Bye, I'm on my way to meet Marianne."

"Alright, I'll be glad when the study hall thing is over with. Bye."

Ruthie rushed down the drive towards the big tree at the end, blowing gently in the morning breeze, crossed the street and hurried up on Marianne's porch which was littered with dog things, a bed, toys, and bowl, rang the bell, her brother, Frank, answered the door. "Wow, you're early. Marianne, Ruthie is here."

"Okay, coming."

Frank said, "Come on in."

Ruthie stepped into a tiny hall at the foot of a stairway as Marianne came down the stairs looking disheveled. Her hair looked quickly combed and her lipstick looked crooked. "Gosh, I'm a mess. You are really early, what's the rush?"

"I have a lot to tell you, and I can't wait."

They got outside on the sidewalk and headed toward Hancock Street. "Marianne, I don't think I care much about Joe anymore. Remember when I mentioned I was flunking Latin and I didn't know what to do? Well, Miss Clark set it up with Mr. Phillips for me to go to the study hall for extra study. Mr. Phillips arranged for Jim Keelon to help me. I have flipped out over him. He's not the person people think he is. He is very good looking, is very smart and has a great sense of caring about other people."

Marianne said, "Hold on. How many times has he helped you?"

"Twice."

"Oh, twice, that's really getting to know someone. You know like talking maybe a total of twenty minutes in a study hall. Give me a break."

"I know it sounds crazy, especially since he has been dating Marie Calhoun."

"Oh, that's perfect. You don't need the headache from her again. Emily is going to flip, another Catholic boy. You're asking for it, this time. Last week nobody could match Joe. He was the best third baseman, handsome, tall and had the best personality, wow what a change."

They reached the halfway mark towards school, the stadium.

Ruthie said, "I know it's a complete change, but it's a feeling I have, Jim is soft spoken, polite, handsome and nice, I'm convinced, what else can I say?"

They reached the schoolyard. Marianne said, "You don't have to say anything. Here comes Marie and behind her is the man of the hour, Jim. This should set the day off good." Marie looked gorgeous, as usual, in a light blue skirt and sweater with matched angora socks. Ruthie already felt defeated.

Marie stepped closer and said, "Well if it isn't the Latin student and man chaser."

Ruthie said, "It's not what you think, I have to pass Latin and I am desperate for the extra help."

"You're desperate all right, but not the way you're pretending. First it was Frank, then Joe, and now it's Jim. You're getting boy crazy."

Jim stepped closer and said, "Hi everyone." He was wearing black slacks, a blue checked shirt and a light gray jacket. Ruthie's heart jumped a little.

He said to Ruthie, "Wow that color looks good on you. Don't forget the study hall later."

"Thanks, I won't. I worked on what we talked about so I'm getting caught up."

Marie interrupted, "Jim, remember Friday. Is it still on?"

"I'm not sure. I might not be able to get the car."

Marie said, "You're last in line, Frank, then Joe and now you.

Doesn't that bother you? Good luck." Jim shrugged and said, "Whatever."

Ruthie was elated. Maybe Jim is dropping Marie. She said nothing.

Then the bell for first class rang. Everyone began to scatter. Marie was the first to run.

Marianne said, "Isn't she pathetic? Look at her run. Saved again by the bell."

Chapter 50

Ruthie was weaving her way through the crowded corridor towards the study hall. A girl, Joan, very popular with the in crowd grabbed Ruthie's hand and said, "I would like to talk to you. Let's move to the side of the corridor." Ruthie said, "Okay." They moved near a wall on the side. Joan, a pretty brunette dressed in a navy plaid dress said, "Do you study with Jim Keelon?" Ruthie said, "Yes, I got behind in Latin and Mr. Phillips asked Jim to catch me up. Why?" "Well, I heard he is going to ask you to the prom and Marie Calhoun told somebody if that happens she plans to ruin your reputation. I wanted you to know, because she already did it to me, she makes up lies that kind of thing." Ruthie shook her head disgustedly and said, "What next, angrily. She said, "Well I need the extra studying, because I cannot fail Latin. If I do, I won't graduate. If he asks me, I might say yes. Thanks for warning me; I have to get going to the study hall."

"Well, she told different guys that I went to the cemetery at night and knew all the best places to hide and get undressed. She called my mom and told her the same things. I hope it doesn't happen to you."

Ruthie opened the study hall door; Jim was already there. He looked extra nice, in a blue blazer with a white shirt opened at the collar. A few desks away, Joe, dressed in a faded baseball jersey, was reading and writing in a notebook.

Ruthie, at first didn't know which way to turn, but she walked straight towards Jim and said, "Hey, I have a problem, can you excuse me for a minute?"

"Yeah, sure, I see it. Take your time. Go ahead."

Ruthie slowly approached Joe and merely said, "Hi. I thought you had baseball practice."

"Yeah, I do but I have some homework I have to finish. Then, I'm going to the field. I'm playing third for the school team. I don't see you much anymore."

"I know, I got so far behind in Latin, Miss Clark set it up with Mr. Phillips to get some tutoring from another classmate."

"So, I heard." He collected his things and got up to leave. He said in his ever-present diffident manner, "I guess I'll see you around." He shrugged one shoulder, stood up and said, "So long."

Ruthie spoke softly, "Yeah, so long. Good luck on the team."

He left. Ruthie walked back to her desk beside Jim.

Jim said, "Everything okay? You used to go with him didn't you? Or do you still?"

"Naw, we kind of broke it off. I did go with him, but it was always me making the effort and I didn't like that. It's his personality. He's heavy into sports, all sports."

"Good. Are you going to the prom?" He pushed his chair back a little as if to move nearer.

Ruthie felt her face get hot and red, but she managed to blurt out, "I want to, I guess it was assumed I would go with Joe, but that's not possible, now."

Jim touched her arm lightly and said, "How about going with me?"

Ruthie's heart beat so fast, she was afraid it would show through Beth's sweater. "Gosh, that would be fun, yes."

Jim squeezed her hand.

Mr. Phillips, his fat stomach jiggling and his wire glasses hanging on his nose approached and said, "If you two have all your social activities settled, I want to see you studying."

They said in unison, "Yes, we are."

Ruthie rattled off some conjugations that she had been practicing. Jim said, "Wow, you did great."

"I better, the final is next Wednesday."

"Okay, let's review some tenses and next Tuesday when we come back, we'll review."

They worked until four thirty, picked up their materials, said good-bye to Mr. Phillips and walked to the schoolyard.

When they were out of the building, Ruthie said, "Joan Holmes told me you were going to ask me to the prom and she said Marie Calhoun threatened to ruin my reputation with lies if it happened."

"She's good at that, just ignore it, if you can, don't give her the satisfaction it bothers you."

Ruthie said, "I'll try."

"I'm telling you, you'll play into her hands if she realizes she won by getting to you. I have my dad's car, do you want a ride home?"

"Gee, that would be great."

"We can kill two birds with one stone, I can find out where you live when I pick you up for prom night."

Ruthie's face got hot again and, her heart jumped. again. A little voice inside reminded of Marie, but right then she was too excited.

Chapter 51

When Ruthie walked through the kitchen, she looked and saw that Emily was in the dining room knitting in the sunlight by the dining room window. Ruthie decided that was a good time to tell her about Jim Keelon, because when Emily had been knitting she was usually relaxed. Ruthie figured she'd have to face it in any case.

She put her chin on the top of her hands. Bowed her head and rested them on her chest. She was nervous about telling Emily, but decided to just blurt it out. "Emily, I have something to tell you. I met a new boy who has been helping me to pass Latin. He asked me to the prom and I said yes. His name is Jim Keelon."

"Oh? Is that the huge Irish Catholic family living down near the beach? Great. You're at it again. No, you can't go. Tell him I said, no."

Ruthie's eyes filled. "Please, Emily. He's nice, he's president of the senior class."

"No, period. I don't care if he's King Tut." Emily stood putting her knitting in the bag. She tucked the needles in, zipped the bag, and set it in the chair.

Ruthie buried her head in her hands, tears rolled down her cheeks as she stood in front of Emily and cried hard.

Harry walked in from work still carrying his thermos and said, "What's going on? I heard you two down in the driveway."

Emily said, "She's wants to go to the prom with another boy from the wrong side of the tracks. I said no. Another Catholic, we don't need any more." Emily straightened her red knit top and tossed her hair back. She looked really skinny.

"Emily, for God sakes, it's just a dance date, let her go." Harry smelled of car grease. He set his black lunch pail on the dining room table. His hair looked too long.

Emily would be on that soon.

Ruthie stopped sniveling and listened.

Emily said, "I suppose you're right, but I want to meet this character before she goes anywhere with him."

Harry turned to Ruthie and said, "Bring him home so we can meet him."

Ruthie hugged Harry and said, "I will. That's a good idea. He'll like meeting you, too." Ruthie made that up to try to give a good impression of Jim.

After supper, Emily said, "We'll have to fix a dress for you. Charlotte has one that we can try, and if it doesn't work, we'll buy you one."

Ruthie said, "Does that mean I can go?"

Emily said, "Yes, unless this kid turns out to be a Mafia person or terribly rude."

Ruthie said, "You will like him. I know you will. She rubbed her hands and them wiggled them as she said, "He's quiet, friendly and polite, and he's tall with dark hair and light blue eyes."

"Hmm, typical description of an Irish kid."

Harry, reading the newspaper, sitting nearby still in his work clothes said, "Ok, that's enough." Emily figured what religion a kid was by his name. Kelly, Hughes, Sullivan etc. made them Catholic and Irish. Balducci, Sachetti, DeTroia etc. made them Italian and Catholic. It was immediate dislike with Emily, and it made them come from the wrong side of the tracks.

Ruthie changed the subject towards the prom dress. "I think I know the dress Charlotte has, everyone has worn it to at least one dance, but it's a great dress. It has nice material, watered silk taffeta. I think the buttons are faded, but we could take those off and add some velvet down the front. I really like it."

Emily said, "That's a good idea. Let me think about that."

Beth came into the living room already in her blue robe and her hair in curlers.

"What's going on? Don't tell me; let me guess. Ruthie is going to the prom with Jim Keelon. I guess my royal blue sweater, worked, huh? Poor Joe, she gave him the gate after going to the ball field all the time."

Ruthie said, "Just shut up, it's none of your business."

"What about the summer of love that we heard about night and day? The poor guy might be crying in his baseball mitt right now."

Harry spoke up again, "Okay, enough. Beth if you have homework, get on it. Ruthie, that goes for you, too. Good night."

Beth and Ruthie headed for the stairs to their bedroom. Emily heard Beth say on the way up, "You're something, you know it? I don't know what, but something. Boy crazy for sure."

Chapter 52

The next day in the study hall, Ruthie decided to ask Jim for a ride home, but if he didn't have the car, maybe they could walk home. That might be better anyway, her heart jumped thinking of the walk with him. Wow. She had taken extra care with her hair and had her favorite outfit on, a navy skirt and white sweater.

She walked to the study hall amid the usual corridor noise and who was walking toward her? Joe. He was wearing a worn gray baseball shirt and some old khakis. "Oh no, I don't need this." He didn't even look at her, but turned towards some other baseball players, also in the hall.

Ruthie waved, he looked but didn't wave back, completely unmindful. She took a deep breath. Raised her eyebrows and said to herself, "Typical Joe, more interested in sports." She hurried past the gathering. One in the crowd, Babe, yelled, "Hey, Ruthie." Joe didn't care; Babe was an instigator and a wiseguy.

She turned and waved. Then she turned her mind to Jim waiting in the study hall.

In front of the study hall, she fixed her hair on the sides, and then opened the door, Jim wasn't there. The study hall looked different, most of the books had been removed, probably for summer. The shades were drawn all the way down. Mr. Phillips said, "Ruthie. May I see you, please?" He was sitting behind his desk, no glasses on, and said, abruptly, "More personal business. Jim couldn't make it today. He left this. He handed Ruthie a note."

Ruthie took the white folded note. Jim had a dentist appointment. When she finished reading it, she moved closer to Mr. Phillip's desk and said, "Thank you for all you did to help me. This was going to be the last time, and I wanted you to know it was a big help. I hope you have a nice summer."

Mr. Phillips put on his wire glasses and stood up. "You're very welcome. Ruthie. I hope you pass and graduate with your class."

Ruthie turned to leave. A million thoughts flooded her mind. How am I going to set up the meeting with Emily? Then she decided the Latin test was more important. Then she thought about Joe completely ignoring her. What about Babe shouting hi? He was put up to it.

She decided to take a chance and go to see Miss Clark, somehow that might make her feel better about the upcoming test. Her door was closed. Ruthie gently knocked and Miss Clark said, "Come in." All the maps and pictures had been taken down for summer. The room looked bare. Miss Clark was at her desk wearing the yellow green dress with the dirtiest belt. "Yes, Ruthie, what is it? I'm in a hurry."

Ruthie drew her lips back, let out her breath and said, bashfully, "I wanted to tell you thank you for suggesting the study hall tutoring. I feel like I learned a lot."

"Good, the test is tomorrow. Study hard tonight. Now, if that's it, I have to go."

"Okay, bye, Miss Clark." She left and closed the door behind her. She couldn't believe Miss Clark almost pushed her away. That might be good. I'll make sure I pass with a good grade,

As she walked toward the schoolyard, she heard Jim calling, "Hey, Ruthie, wait. I'm sorry I couldn't make it today, I had a dentist appointment I forgot about."

He was wearing Levis and a faded navy tee shirt. He looked handsome. Ruthie said, "Oh, it's okay, I thanked Mr. Phillips and Miss Clark for the extra help. I think I will pass after I brush up tonight. Is there anyway you can drive me home? My sister wants to meet you before the prom. She's fussy."

"Sure, I have the car." He squeezed her hand. Ruthie was sure he could hear her heart thump.

As they approached the car, Jim opened the door for her. When he closed it, Ruthie looked out the window and saw Marie Calhoun running towards them. Ruthie actually felt angry and wanted to scream at Marie.

Marie yelled out loudly, enough so Ruthie heard through the window, "Jim, what are you doing? Don't you know you are headed for trouble? Ruthie Brooks is a tramp. She went to the baseball field in West Quincy and necked behind the bleachers with Joe almost everyday. No telling what else they did."

Jim stepped away from the car a little. Ruthie lowered the window. Jim put up both of his hands and said, "Marie, stop. Don't you ever get sick of causing trouble? I know you're telling a bunch of lies right now. I don't want to hear anymore, period."

Marie lowered her head and tried to save face. "Where are you going, now, to the baseball bleachers?"

Jim walked to the driver's side of the car and got in. Ruthie was crying. Jim patted her shoulder and said, "Well, at least you know what is going to be spread around. Joan never found out until the lies were really out there. Be glad you don't do that stuff."

Ruthie stopped crying and said, "You're right, but it still stings and makes me angry. I'm going to have to make myself forget it."

Jim started the car and said, "Okay, let's go meet your sister. I hope this isn't a preview of how that will go."

"Yeah." Ruthie looked out the window and wished for her mother. Wouldn't it be nice if she were taking Jim to meet her mother? Her mother with her soft smile and voice would listen and be sympathetic.

Chapter 53

Jim got behind the wheel and turned toward Ruthie. He touched her shoulder and said, "Are you okay? Are we still going to meet your sister?"

"Yes, I'm okay. Thank you for taking my part with Marie. And, yes, my sister is waiting to meet you. I told her I would bring you home with me after school today."

"Hey, I have told you a million times not to play into her hands. It makes her feel special. So, where do I go?"

"Go straight down Hancock St. until we get to Wollaston and then I'll give you the street directions."

Ruthie said, "I think I will do okay on the Latin test. I know I'll pass. I'd like to get at least a B.

But any passing grade will be great. My sister thinks taking languages is a big waste of time so if I fail, I'll be doing what you said, playing into her hands. That's worse than with Marie."

"Gee, maybe it's not such a good ides to meet her."

"It'll work out, turn here and go straight down Elm Avenue until you get to Sycamore Street, turn right. It's 134."

When they arrived at Ruthie's house, Ruthie took his hand and led him up the steps to the front porch. Emily had put so big potted flowers there. One was a large clay pot filled with huge sunflowers, the other flowers, Ruthie didn't recognize. Emily opened the door. She had on a light gray skirt and red sweater, her wimpy hair was casually brushed back, and it even looked good.

Ruthie introduced Jim. Although, he was dressed in a faded shirt and Levis, Ruthie could tell he was not what Emily expected. In fact, Emily was flustered; she cleared her throat, attempted a cough and said, "Gee, it's nice meeting you. Come in."

They entered the living room and she said, "Sit down. I'll get some cookies that I just baked."

Ruthie never expected this nice welcome and Emily's chocolate chip cookies were the best.

Jim looked at Ruthie. Raised his eyebrows, winked and gave a low-key thumbs up as Emily left the room.

Emily was back quickly with a tray of cookies that she placed on the coffee table. She sat on the opposite side of the room.

"Help yourself"

Jim and Ruthie each took one. Jim said, "Wow, these are delicious."

Emily spoke first. "Ruthie told me you helped her with Latin. I am not sure languages do any good out in the world, unless maybe a person is considering translating as a line of work."

Jim said. "Well Latin is a good basis for most languages. It helps find meanings with English words. For example gratitude comes from Latin, gratus, meaning thankful. I can't think of a lot of them now, but Latin has helped me figure out meanings many times."

"I never looked at it from that angle. That would be a help."

Ruthie could see Emily was pleased with Jim.

Jim glanced at his watch and said, "I really enjoyed the visit and especially the cookies, but I have to pick up my brother, Charlie at 5. It was nice to have met you and I hope I see you again, soon."

Emily said, "I enjoyed it, myself."

Ruthie walked to the front door, said goodbye and mentioned she would study the Latin that night.

She turned to Emily and said, "Do you like him? Can I go to the prom with him?"

Emily said, "Yes. You need a new dress. He is very polite and extremely handsome."

For the first time, Ruthie ran to Emily, squeezed her neck and said, "Thank you, thank you, Emily."

She headed up to her room and on the way thought about her mother who would have been proud of how nice Emily had been.

She said to herself, a new dress, Emily liking Jim, graduation, it was almost too much.

Chapter 54

The next morning, Ruthie woke at six. She felt like she had tossed around all night. She kept thinking about the Latin test at eleven o'clock. The night before she studied until ten, reviewing the things Jim had taught her and the things from class. Her stomach made a funny noise as she looked out the window on what looked like a gloomy day. Her was a tossed mess, and she had an old faded blue nightgown on. She laughed and thought if Jim could see her now, he'd probably consider taking Marie to the prom after all.

She got up and headed towards the bathroom. Beth groaned and said, "Be quiet. Just because you're getting up with the birds, doesn't mean you have to rummage around and wake me."

"Shut up, all you do is complain, I am being quiet."

Ruthie went to the closet to get her gray skirt and pink sweater. Beth spoke again, "You're not wearing anything of mine."

"I took the pink sweater."

"Oh, alright, but you wear it so much, the kids will think it's yours."

Ruthie headed down the stairs to wash her hair and take a bath. Then she went to the kitchen where Emily was sitting in the gloom drinking coffee. Emily said, "I guess you're nervous about the Latin test, huh? That's why you're up so early?"

"Yes, but I think it will go good. I don't want to eat anything, just juice."

To Ruthie's surprise, Emily agreed.

Ruthie planned to go to the Latin classroom early and beg Miss Clark to correct her paper while she waited. Her stomach jumped a little, because she was afraid Miss Clark might say no and that meant Ruthie would have to wait until the next class, two days away.

She said, "I'm going to finish getting dressed." She headed to the stairway.

Emily called her back, "Ruthie, I wish you good luck on your test."

"Gee, thank you for that, Emily. You made me feel great."

Wow, Ruthie thought as she ruffled her hands through her damp hair, Emily is really being nice to me. Maybe that's a good sign. She never did anything like that before.

Maybe Harry had a talk with her. Maybe it's because she liked Jim who knows she runs hot and cold, but it feels good.

She dressed in the pink sweater, combed her hair, which looked pretty good. Hmm another good sign.

She went downstairs through the kitchen. Emily evidently had enough coffee; she was in her bedroom making her bed.

Ruthie yelled, "Bye, I am leaving, I'll see you this afternoon."

"Okay, bye. Have a good day."

What a switch, Emily actually wishing her a good day.

Ruthie hurried down the stairs, down the driveway towards Marianne's house. Queenie, Marianne's dog met her and they walked towards Marianne's.

Frank, Marianne's answered the door. He was wearing a torn gray robe and is hair was a greasy mess. He acted as bad a he looked. "God, what are you doing here? Are you trying to outdo the milkman? Come in, I suppose. Marianne just got up."

"I'm sorry, I have a test and I have to be early."

He ushered her to the living room. "Have a seat. I'll get Marianne."

Ruthie sat in a corner on a pretty soft striped chair. The room had a white fireplace and was decorated with matching chairs and a sofa. Much prettier than Emily's and cozier.

Marianne came into the room not long after Ruthie.

She said, "I'm a mess." He hair was still quite wet, but the rest of her appearance was neat. She was wearing a new yellow sweater and black skirt,"

Ruthe said, "Wow, you look nice."

Marianne said, "Thanks, I coaxed my Dad into buying it."

When they got outside, they were surprised by the change in the weather, the sun was out, the dampness was gone and it looked like it was going to be a good day after all. They started on their walk to school.

Chapter 55

The sun started to come out turning the weather into a cool spring day. Marianne said, "I guess you're worried about the Latin test, huh?"

"Sort of, but it's the usual nervousness about any test. Actually, I have studied hard, and I feel deep inside I will pass with at least a B."

"Gee, Jim must have helped."

Ruthie laughed, "Yeah, in more ways than one. I got the help I needed, and I am going to the prom with him."

"That's great. The next time I want a good date, I think I'll ask for help in the study hall."

They both laughed as they approached the half way mark, the stadium.

Ruthie said, "Just think we'll be graduating here next month. Are you going down the cape this summer?"

"I think so. I hope Emily will let you come down for a week."

"I can't think about that now, I'll tackle that one later. You know how she is about Beth and I doing the housework and going to the store."

"What does she do all day? Read books?"

"Washing."

"All day?"

"Yeah. Incredible isn't it?"

They arrived at the schoolyard. Jim was there with a bunch of the guys. There were small bunches of kids everywhere.

Jim left his crowd and came over to Marianne and Ruthie. Ruthie's heart thumped. He had on a gray sweater and jeans. His hair was slightly tossed. He said, "Hey. Are you nervous? You can do it."

The bell rang for homeroom class. Kids from all around the schoolyard headed for the door to the hallway.

Ruthie said, "No, I'm not any more nervous than for any other test. Thanks to you. I think I'll ask Miss Clark to glance over my final to see if I passed. She knows how much it means. I have to hurry, bye."

"Okay, good luck. See you at lunch."

In her homeroom, Ruthie thought about her mother and Huff's Neck. She was far away with her mother at the pier with Jake giving them fish when Miss Cash called her name for attendance. She finally heard her name and said, "Here."

Miss Cash said, "For awhile I thought you were in Boston."

The class laughed out loud.

Finally homeroom was dismissed. Ruthie was on her way to take the Latin test. She walked slowly and was the last one out.

As she headed down the hall, she didn't even hear all the noise or kids saying hi, her nerves had set in. She fidgeted with her hair and kept fixing her books.

When she arrived at Miss Clark's room, Joe was already there. He whispered, "Hey, don't worry, you'll pass. Good luck."

Ruthie smiled and said, "Thanks. Shocked at his friendly attitude.

Miss Clark passed the test papers. Ruthie kept saying to herself, "I, isti, it, imus, istis, erunt."

The class was given thirty minutes for the test.

When Miss Clark finally said, "Time's up." Ruthie felt good. She hoped that was a good sign.

She waited until everyone left the room before she approached Miss Clark.

Finally Miss Clark looked up and saw her at her desk. "Can I help you, Ruthie?"

"Is there anyway I can get my grade now? I'm sort of in trouble at home." She chewed her pinky fingernail.

"Weelll, I usually don't do that, but I will in your situation."

Ruthie sat at her desk and waited for what seemed like 2 hours, Miss Clark finally said, "C+, you did it."

Ruthie ran to Miss Clark's desk and gave her a hug. Miss Clark had on the dirtiest belt again. She pulled away.

Ruthie left the room, hurried down the empty hall looking for anybody to listen to the news. Nobody was around. Ruthie said to herself, "Mama, I passed the Latin test."

She knew her mother heard because she felt so happy inside.

Chapter 56

In June of 1949, Ruthie was graduating from Quincy High School. Emily had bought her a pink dotted Swiss dress with a wide pink sash. The collar folded over like two large petals. She had low patent leather high heels, too

The graduation was going to be held at the Quincy Stadium. She and Marianne had used this as a measurement for how much time they had without being late for school.

Ruthie was excited because her sisters, their husbands, Mim and a few other friends were to be there to see her get her diploma.

The night was warm and clear. Ruthie tried not to think about her mother's death and that all of her friends would have their parents there. Most of her close friends were nice and never mentioned her mother's death.

One thing that bothered Ruthie about the upcoming event was the distribution of the diplomas.

Mr. Wilson, the principal, had said, "We just give them out as they are stacked. It's up to each of you to locate the student who has yours."

She thought what if I couldn't find mine?

Then she consoled herself; it'll at least be in the school office.

Emily interrupted her thoughts, "Ruthie. Come down here so I can make sure your outfit looks right. If it needs adjusting, we still have time to do that."

"Coming. I'm almost dressed."

Ruthie had struggled with her hair. She wore it loosely with a tiny braid down one side.

She went into the living room dressed in her dress and shoes.

Emily looked her and handed her a small box from the flower shop in Wollaston and said, "These are for you."

Ruthie removed the cover and sniffed the sweet smell of the two gardenias nestled in green paper. She said, "Oh, they are perfect. Thank you."

A real tear slid down Emily's face as she confessed, "You look so nice and you have made me so proud of you. Thank you for being easy to raise."

She reached out and actually hugged Ruthie and continued, "Tonight is going to be perfect. I think we'll feel like a real family as we all sit together and then go out to eat."

"Thank you, Emily. It will be." Six thirty finally came. Emily, Harry and Ruthie went down stairs to get into their coupé. Ruthie climbed into the back seat.

Harry settled into the driver's seat and said, "I hope we can find a decent place to park. I think we will because we're leaving a little early."

Everyone was quiet on the way to the stadium. When they arrived, an attendant directed them to the parking area. Everything was orderly. Ruthie could see folding chairs on the field where the graduates would be sitting.

A light summer breeze blew as the three of them walked to meet the others in their group.

Beth ran towards Ruthie and said, "Wow, what a dress. And flowers You look better than anyone here. Let me smell." She sniffed the two gardenias pinned to Ruthie's dress.

Ruthie said, "Thanks. I like it, myself."

Charlotte and her husband had brought Mim who said, "My, Ruthie, I am very happy and proud."

Ruthie stepped towards her and squeezed her hand. She turned to everyone and said, "I better be getting down on the field before Mr. Wilson sees me up here." Everywhere she looked she saw her classmates dressed up, the guys in suits and the girls in pretty dresses. All the seniors walked onto the field to the tune of "Pomp and Circumstance."

Shortly after all were seated, one of the Kilbourne twins recited a brief farewell to the class.

Mr. Jack, the biology teacher, gave the commencement address.

The admonition was from Robert Browning, "Ah, but a man's reach should exceed his grasp, or what's a heaven for?"

Barbara, a friend sitting near Ruthie, said, "You're sisters just sat down. I know it's them, because they have picture hats on. They're the fanciest ones here."

Ruthie laughed.

The achievement awards were given and after that the diplomas were distributed. The class was nearly 200, so that took some time.

Ruthie thought of her mother and how pleased she would be if she could be here. She remembered her mother's empty hospital bed with her magazine and the asters with other belongings lying in the center.

Her memories were interrupted Mr. Wilson holding her diploma. called, "Ruthie Brooks." Ruthie stepped forward, smiled and said "Thank you." Inside she whispered, "Mama, I did it."